LINGERLUST
By Matt Smart

LINGERLUST

Written by

Matt Smart

Copyright © 2021 Matt Smart

No part of this book may be used or reproduced by any means, graphic, electronic, or mechanical, including photocopying, recording, taping or by any information storage retrieval system without the express permission o the author, except in the case of brief quotations embodied in the critical articles and reviews. This is a work of fiction. All of the characters, names, incidents, organisations and dialogues in the novel are the products of the authors imagination or are used fictitiously, except where listed in the notes section in the back. Some concepts in this book have been influenced by urban legend or reported yet unproven events. Any similarity to persons living or dead is purely coincidental, except those listed in the notes section.

"Think about it. If you travel to the past, that past becomes your future. And your former present becomes the past, which can't now be changed by your new future."

— The Hulk

For my children - Ollie and Leo

It has always been my dream to write and publish a fiction story, and thanks to my wonderful family and the best friends anyone can wish for, I have finally made my dream come true.

Prologue

Planet Earth - Leading up to the year 2775

The future is a wonderful, peaceful utopia. The past of the future is a catastrophic demolition of civilisation as we know it.

By the year 2775, Humans have, for centuries colonised the Moon, Mars and to some extent Venus and Mercury. Back in 2032 a relatively new private space agency called SpaceX sent the first humans to Mars. These pioneers were able to harness various local resources on Mars and by using equipment delivered in different missions, they were also able to '3D print' primitive habitats. From there, they harboured natural resources like carbon dioxide, iron, aluminium, silicon and sulphur, which could be used to make things like glass, brick and plastic. And with a little work, they could even use the planet's hydrogen and methanol to create rocket fuel for return trips back to earth. The moon was undergoing a similar colonisation but was a preferred location outside of planet earth for the military, consequently very few civilians lived on the moon and what was being built there, was extremely secretive.

By 2059 there were almost ten thousand humans living on the surface or Mars in huge colonies, each spanning over one hundred kilometres across. There were shops, houses, highways and even sports grounds. The sports grounds were mostly used for Athletics tournaments and competitions such as light-sabre fencing, low gravity gymnastics and e-sports. Ball based sports were banned at this time as there were numerous incidents of damages and injuries caused by many golf balls, many of which had been struck from at least 12 kilometres away.

In the year 2185, Asteroid (410777) 2009 FD, a 500 metre wide lump of iron which was first discovered back in 2009, smashed into the Atlantic ocean sending unimaginably large tsunamis ripping outwards towards the Americas and the European continents. One hundred metre waves crashed into cities and towns wiping out millions of people in an instant. The atmosphere heated up to immense temperatures, triggering forest fires and roasting anything not sheltered deep underground. The combination of dust from the impact and soot from the forest fires remained in the Earth's atmosphere for more than three years, blocking most the light of the Sun. Without sunlight, much of the Earth's plant life, on land and in the sea, died. Over a million species of animals were made extinct and over 85% of the global population was lost.

Leading up to the year 2392, humanity had managed to pick itself back up and with a population now up to one billion and an advancing technology rivalling that of 2019 it looked like the human race might eventually fully recover from the 'Great one' in 2185. But, by the time 2392 had come around, the planet was on the brink of a major global war. A war that had started over the rights to various fishing lanes. Fishing lanes at this time had become a highly sort-after prize, as most of the fish had completely disappeared since the 'big one' and never really recovered. So the price of certain types of fish, which once were very affordable, were now out of reach for even some of the wealthiest, even for a single fillet. At the end of 2392, nuclear war finally broke out. It was brief, deadly and left no more than 300 million human beings on planet earth. Life for the survivors was unbearable for generations to come. Radiation contamination lasted hundreds of years and killed in minutes.

At around this time, which most people estimated to be about 2650, anti-gravity was discovered. The relatively small human population had learned to live with each other and love one another unlike at any time in history. Schools were non existent, in fact they were even deemed completely unnecessary as teaching became something that every citizen was obliged to do. Children and adults alike were taught anywhere and everywhere by anyone and everyone. Most teachings consisted of the usual maths and sciences, but there was also an emphasis on understanding what it meant to be a human being on planet earth. They would be taught the terrible history of this planet and understand how the people who went before us sacrificed so much so the future generations can see how life should be lived and loved. There was no crime, though of course altercations did occur, but these were usually quickly resolved and therefore there was no need for any kind of police force. Money is by now long obsolete and citizens of planet earth are allocated credits as rewards for their deeds - thee included teaching, cleaning, healing or any kind of social activity that benefited humankind. Hospitals were free and open, as humans had learned how to harness the energy of the universe. Healing was done with light and energy.

However, during this time, ground radiation was still a major problem so due to the introduction of anti-gravity cities and towns were now being built in the skies. They floated on gigantic platforms which mimicked the earths gravity and reversed it perfectly. Of course one big bonus with having floating cities was that you could move them. You could move them to anywhere in the world, raising or lowering them to any height necessary. Sunny days were guaranteed, unless of course the intercity artificial intelligence systems deemed it important that everyone should get wet and therefore proceeded to lower the city underneath a nice rain cloud. Trips down to the surface were allowed, but for the most part no one was particularly interested. Sometimes some citizens would organise a history tour of sunken New York, or the Forest of London. Protective clothing was worn at all times and they would always be safe travelling inside a reinforced Tesla Skycar.

There was one particular group of people however, an organisation to be exact, who had built themselves a base under the surface of planet earth. They were a militant group who had mostly been born into the organisation, consequently some families had been a part of the organisation for five or six generations. They also had a headquarters on the moon but in truth, most of their operations were conducted underground. This organisation was known as The Logistics of Interplanetary Nucleosynthesis and General Elemental Research or L.I.N.G.E.R. Most were completely unaware of this organisation, others dismissed them as conspiracy theory or just another urban legend. LINGER was not necessarily interested in the welfare of their fellow humans, health, education or anything that might truly benefit them. They were interested in one thing and one thing alone, power.

As far back as 1954, the United States Air Force had reported that a satellite orbiting the earth had been detected. Of course at this time, no country had the technology to launch a satellite into orbit, so the detection was mostly dismissed as an error, conspiracy or even plain lies. This satellite was given the nickname 'The Black Knight' probably due to the British rockets at the time called Black Knight Rockets, but in truth, the existence of this satellite resides with LINGER. In the year 2745 they had secretly developed time travel technology, which needed the use of a satellite orbiting the planet that you wanted to time travel within. So they developed the Black Knight Satellite, put it into orbit and then sent it back through time roughly thirteen thousand years. So, as long as this satellite is in existence, they are able to travel back to any point in earth's history with extreme accuracy.

LINGER now, have every intention of using this immensely powerful and extremely dangerous technology for their own gain.

ONE

AD 2019 - May 30 - Charlie

Something was clearly off when I arrived at work that morning. Kate's French tips would usually be pounding away at her keyboard while she smacked her gum between her teeth from behind her desk. On a typical day she would have never greeted me at all. If I was lucky, maybe a nod of her head to acknowledge my existence, or maybe a very brief moment of eye contact before she pretended to be busy again. All in all, she was truly a remarkable receptionist.

Today however, I felt her eyes as soon as I came through the door. I thought maybe there was some kind of mustard stain on my suit or something. It was noticeably quiet as I turned and gave Kate an awkward, "Good morning," but it sounded much more like a question than a greeting.

"Ah, hey, good morning Charlie, Mr. Butler needs you in his office, like, pronto. He said he needed to see you before you got started for the day." She popped a small bubble from the gum in her mouth and then was then face down in her computer once more.

Okay, that didn't seem too weird. Mr. Butler wasn't the line manager who I typically worked under, but he was the one who hired me for the job. I gave Kate a nod, which she obviously didn't see, before making my way to his office. My social life had kind of been in the shitter since moving to London and Kate was always a great reminder of that. I hadn't met too many people in London outside of work that I'd really became friends with. However, my professional life was thriving, I was working for a company that I loved and I'm sure they loved me back, and that in itself was more than enough to keep me going.

"Charlie, You're fired."

That was it. That was why Mr. Butler wanted to see me. He didn't even look up from the papers he was studying. The muted sounds of keyboards, copy machines and telephones came from outside of his office filled the uncomfortable moment before I replied.

"Pardon me?" It came out way more pitiful than I would have hoped.

"Charlie," he finally looked up from the papers, rubbing his shiny bald head and leaning back in his expensive chair, "I don't even want to ask what the hell happened, what were you thinking to do something so utterly harebrained. But at the same time you've caused me too much trouble over the weekend, so as much as I would like to say I don't really care, I do have to ask as the company takes the release of sensitive information extremely seriously — Would you like to tell me exactly why you decided to upload Ana's client's banking information onto social media and god only knows where else for the entire planet to see?"

My breath caught in my throat for a second, "Woah, seriously? Mr. Butler, I would honestly never even think about releasing any sensitive information—"

"Really Charlie? But You did. See here? Uploaded by Charlie Anderson," Mr. Butler slapped the papers down in front of me on his much too big desk so I could see the evidence for myself.

"But there's just no way," I moved closer to confirm for myself. Yep, sure enough, account numbers, bank codes and even names and addresses, confirmed and uploaded by Charlie Anderson, seriously? What the hell? In desperation, I tried for a moment to think of some other person I might know called Charlie Anderson that might be able to take the blame for this, but no, it's just me. Surely, I had to have done this while sleep walking, or under some kind of hypnosis, because I had really no recollection of even logging in to the system on that day, "Sir, Mr. Butler, I'm so sorry, I really don't understand how this could've happened, can you please let me try and fix —"

"No, Charlie, unfortunately for you, this isn't a slap on the wrist type of scenario, kid. In fact, I'd go as far as to say that the company are very much considering suing you for this, not my idea but you know what they are like, so please don't dig yourself a deeper hole. Now listen, I need to you go back to your desk, get your stuff, exit the building without talking to anyone and leave your work pass with Kate at the front desk, she's expecting it. Would you like me to arrange for someone to escort you out?"

"Um, no that's ok, no escort needed thanks, I'll make my own way out." My head was spinning from the confusion. I clenched my jaw shut to stop me from saying something stupid, then cleared my throat and apologised. I left his office and found my tiny area in the corner of the open plan office with the small desk. I didn't have much stuff really, some writing pads, a pair of squeaky scissors, a few marker pens and a picture of Dad from when I was younger. I was pretty much able to tuck everything away safely in my laptop bag. I could feel my *former* co-worker's eyes on me, some with sorrow, others with anger, others with a strange mix of both. I felt like I wasn't going to be able to breathe again until I left the building. It was a moment that seemed to move in slow-motion yet I barely seem have any recollection of it at all. On my way out, I put my pass on Kate's desk in front of her, obviously she neglected to say goodbye, or even look up at me.

I decided to walk back to my flat. I needed some time to clear my head and didn't want to get on a crowded and smelly underground train, nor did I fancy spending any money on an Uber. The sky was clear and the sun was bright, but it was merely a façade of nice weather. The reality of the day was that there was an unruly wind that was howling through the city resulting in most people walking around with their shoulders up by their ears. I swore the weather was a metaphor for my life here in London so far. It looked wonderful from a window, but you definitely didn't want to be standing in it for too long.

As I walked, I checked my phone for any companies that might be hiring, TWBA Consulting hired me as a paid intern because I was cheap, young and pretty much willing to work any hour of the day or night, they loved that. Working for them really felt like winning the lottery for me. They had free lunches every day, served right to your desk if you wanted it, a fridge full of beers, wines and other alcoholic beverages I'd yet to be introduced to which was also free for everyone — after 5pm. But now, all that was gone. My heart sank even further when I saw there were no new notifications for me. There was still nothing from Noelle, I had called her on Saturday morning to see if she wanted to get some lunch, but I kept getting her voicemail. Finally on the third call she picked up and after asking why the hell I was calling her, told me she never wanted to see or hear from me again. So I'm not sure why I was expecting any messages from her anyway.

I've had a lot of friends and girls come and go during my time here in London, but Noelle lasted the longest and definitely loved the hardest. We were seeing each other for the better half of four months and losing her didn't make sense to me in the slightest. The last time we spoke she was telling me all about her new found love for dark chocolate, something I have a little bit of addiction to myself. So now I'm ghosted by Noelle and thrown out of my job. Is this just how it was here? Were people that much different? I definitely wasn't from the countryside, but I also wasn't used to the city with a population in the millions. Maybe it *was* normal to just throw people out whenever it suits, there's a million more replacements.

Suddenly I noticed a sharp pain on the side of my foot that made me finally look away from my phone. There was something stuck in my shoe. I propped myself up on the side of the closest shop and dug out the imposter. A pebble, shiny and smooth, but still uncomfortable. I gave a quick glance around the smooth and clean pavement and couldn't for the life of me figure out where on earth a pebble this size could have come from?

"So this is what I get for trying to lower my carbon footprint, huh?" I tossed the rock on the pavement, but before I kept walking, I realised I was leaning on one of the windows of The Timber-yard Cafe. This was the coffee shop that I had taken Noelle on our first date. I swallowed hard before deciding to go inside. I was miserable, and misery loves company after all.

I pushed the wooden door open, the lazy sound of a bell chimed briefly as I walked in. The smell of coffee beans and old books perked something inside of me, probably my caffeine addiction. The shop was clean and plastered in fliers and art from all walks of life. I liked it here, it felt almost homely. I greeted the barista and ordered my cappuccino before taking a seat at a round coral table. The sunlight spilled in through the tall windows, and it actually felt warm on the inside.

Within a couple of minutes, the bearded young barista who took my order walked over and handed me my cup wrapped in a napkin. I thanked him, breathing in the brew's wonderful scent. The coffee made me feel happy, but the feeling was short lived as thoughts of Noelle entered my mind again. What did I do that was so terribly wrong? I walked back through my memories of our chats and nights out and found nothing that could warrant her deciding I was the most awful man alive. Looking across the table I could see the memory of her sitting there, smiling at me. Her short blonde locks would've glinted in the sun and she would have smelled like fresh cut flowers.

I grimaced down at my coffee, coming inside the coffee shop might have been a bad idea after all. I twiddled my thumbs on the cup, unfurling the napkin here and there, trying to get my mind to think of something—anything else. It was about this time that I noticed something a bit odd. I opened the napkin and saw scrawled in black ink

'MEET ME OUTSIDE.'

I shot a confused look to the barista, holding up the napkin note. The beard shook its head and shrugged its shoulders. I guessed it wasn't him who wrote it then. I turned to look out of one of the windows to see if there might be any strange looking character out there waiting for me, but I saw nothing but a street cleaner and a busker singing through a traffic cone. My bitter humour made me laugh as I crumpled the napkin, "Well, at least someone around here is wanted."

It probably took me about a half of an hour to get through my whole coffee, I got up and headed for the door turning for a moment to give a nodding goodbye to the barista. When I turned back to the door, a man was outside holding it open for me.

"Oh, thank you," I adjusted my bag's strap over my shoulder as I made a small sprint back outside, trying to hurry out of his way. But he didn't go inside, instead he let the door shut by itself, remaining outside. This is when I got a clear view of him. My stomach gave a sudden jolt of adrenaline and my legs threatened to give way completely. This wasn't just any man. He was me. Or at least, he could've been my identical twin. Or my doppelgänger —

you know they say everyone has one. I stopped dead in my tracks, trying to register the sight of him.

"What's the matter, you don't believe in following instructions?" He pulled at the popped collar of his long black jacket, as if to hide his face.

"Excuse me?" I asked, feeling a bit silly and utterly bewildered.

"The napkin, it said meet me outside," he adjusted his black beanie and shifted his eyes.

"Yeah, the napkin. Do I know you?" I asked.

He shot me an odd look, "Oh, this is gonna be rough."

I took a step back as he began to close the short distance between us, "Listen Charlie, you're in danger, I realise your day is quickly becoming quite the surprise to you, trust me I quite *literally* remember it myself. But you really are in quite a lot of danger and we honestly do need to get out of the open and into somewhere safer. Let's get back to our... um, your place, yeah?"

I know that my instincts should've been to get as far away as possible from the crazy man I've found out on the city streets, but for some reason the adrenaline never came. Inexplicably, I felt I needed to trust this guy. Maybe because he knew my name and I didn't even think to question it. I gave him a quick nod and we began to hurry ourselves to the safety of the 'Luxury Landing Building,' a large high-rise eyesore, which was where where my flat was.

'Luxury' was a stretch that even Elastigirl herself couldn't make. As we got closer to the building, more and more cigarette butts and empty beer bottles littered the road and pavement. They seemed to save the cleaning up for the *nicer* parts of the city. Finally, my building was in sight with its crumbly bricks and run down aluminium gutters. Ah, home sweet home.

We made our way in, the buildings' front door creaking loudly upon opening. The common area was filled with the smell of old ashtrays and a hint of wet dog. I could only thank the heavens that I was able to pay a little extra to be on the ground floor. If I ever had to, I could make a mad dash out of the forsaken place. I struggled briefly with my key in the jingly doorknob before we heard the *click* and we let ourselves in.

My flat was simple and smelt a bit better than the common area. I had a loveseat and a small coffee table that stood upon an old stale rug in the living room next to the back sliding glass door. The walls were plastered with a hideous wallpaper, probably from the 70's and the countertops in the adjacent kitchen were yellow, though I have often wondered whether they used to be white.

"So, can I get you anything? Tea? Coffee?" I set my bag on the coffee table and made my way over towards the kitchen. My guest stood silhouetted in the doorway for what seemed like a whole minute before strolling in further, his hands in his jacket pockets. He kept his bag firmly on his shoulder.

"God, I've always hated this place," he had a grimace as he took in the ambience.

"First of all, it makes a lot of financial sense for me to live here right now. And second of all—what?" I asked.

"Charlie, you may want to get comfortable, maybe change out of that god-awful suit and into some sensible clothes. I have a lot of important info for you and I'm going to need your full attention," his eyes finally made contact with mine.

I felt heat rise from my stomach, "Alright man listen, I don't even know who you are, or why i've randomly decided to let you in my flat, so if it's okay with you I'd love to know what kind of 'danger' I'm in, how you know my name and how you know where I live."

"Ok, I will get straight to the point then. I'm a time traveler, Charlie," he really did cut straight to the point. "Firstly, you can call me Zee, though oddly enough my real name happens to be Charlie. I know exactly how you are feeling right now, you can be certain of that. I am you and you are me, we have made ourselves a very powerful enemy, who may or may not be trying to find us as we speak, actually they probably are, so if I were you, I'd suggest throwing on some sensible clothes—and shoes, while you're at it."

I raised an eyebrow at the man, "Ah. Right, that all makes perfect sense. I feel so much better now, thanks for clearing all that up for me."

"Charlie, I'm serious," his face was flat.

"Come on now, you got any proof of any of this time travel stuff then? Because I would really love to hear it." I folded my arms across my chest, realising that sitting in-front of myself was probably proof enough, though how could I be sitting in-front of myself? The man gave a small huff before finally pulling his hands out of his pockets. He rolled back his jacket sleeve revealing a black leather arm band that almost looked like it could be a smartwatch, but not quite.

The strap was way too thick, but it did have something like a watch face except it was hexagonal. He pushed forward on the face of it with his index finger and a small holographic screen projected from it, hanging in the air. I watched as he used his fingers to scroll through some logs and lists, using the holographic screen as if it were a smartphone.

"Oh my, now that's cool! How does it—"

He cut me off "Charlie, I've very recently travelled from the distant future. You're in danger, real danger, and not only that, anyone you come into contact with is also in danger. I'm here to help you, you know, to give you a fighting chance," the man flicked his wrist and the screen disappeared, "that's why I've done my best to isolate you. I've been able to circumvent your relationships and free you of that job you loved so much."

I eyed the man incredulously, "What! — Exactly, does *that* mean?"

"It means that now you will be able to help me, and I'll be able to help you in return. You will also be temporarily hidden from LINGER."

"Hidden from what? Whats a linger?"

"L.I.N.G.E.R. It Stands for The Logistics of Interplanetary Nucleosynthesis and General Elemental Research, yes, I believe that they are also aware of how ridiculous their name is too, though don't quote me on that. Anyway, they were formed around the turn of the 26th century after the serum which granted immortality was discovered. They are tough and, well yes, kind of immortal. They use what is known as a Stealth Satellite and their knowledge from the future to track people, like you, in the past. Let's just say it won't be so pleasant if they got their hands on you. I have everything you're going to need here." The man finally threw off his bag, unzipped it and started shuffling through the contents, "Let's see now, I've got your portative satellite device. This will communicate with the stealth satellite, which is known as the 'Black Knight' in your time. You will have heard of this as it's a well known conspiracy theory. Except it isn't, it's very much a conspiracy reality. I've also got you a voxer so you can communicate with anyone in any language and also with me as long as we are both in the same time, and—oh man, it's a little archaic, but I have a small notepad with all of the banking information you need for just about any year you go to. For some I reason trust information on paper more than in the kronometer, y'know."

"Wait just a minute, why the hell are these people tracking me? Also, did you say these guys were *immortal*?" I interjected.

"In a sense, yes, there's a serum in my time, a serum that enables people to become immortal. The serum's effect is limited though, so you need a new shot every few hundred years." The man said nonchalantly. "You put the Kronometer on your right wrist and the Voxer on your left, ok". He didn't even look up from his bag.

"—Give me just a sec," I excused myself to the bathroom, my head felt light and I was certain I was going to vomit or pass out, or both. I shut the door behind me and stared at myself in the mirror for a few seconds to gather myself. I grabbed a pair of jeans and wrinkled t-shirt from the floor. Even if this guy was some random crazy person, how did he know so much about my personal life? I thought very briefly about calling the police. I changed my clothes and threw on my old Green Flash shoes in case I had to make a run for it. I ran the tap, splashing cold water over my face, then held both of my hands on the sink as I let the water drip off my skin for a while, steadying my breath. Just then I noticed Noelle's toothbrush beside the tap next to mine. Something hot piqued through me.

I shoved the bathroom door open, stomping back into the main room, "Was it you?" my voice was a guttural.

"Come again?" the man had the pack zipped back up and over his shoulder again.

"Noelle, what did you do with Noelle?" I couldn't control the heat in my chest.

"Oh, the pretty blonde one, I dumped her for you, in person course, I do have some respect. All I did was just tell her things got a little steamy between '*me*' and that receptionist girl. What was her name again? Oh yeah, Kate. Lovely girl," he gave a sarcastic chuckle. I seethed and grabbed him by his jacket's collar.

"Hey wait, wait!" He threw his hands up, "her life was in danger too, Charlie, real *danger*. You cannot be around anybody right now. It will almost certainly bring them harm!"

"Even if that's really the case, why be so cruel to her?" I spat.

"I had to be sure she wouldn't come back," the time traveler sounded sympathetic and somewhat defeated, "This isn't a game Charlie, please understand—"

Suddenly there was an almighty crash, making me jump

and release the man. The door of my flat was smashed open and several men spilled in. I couldn't see exactly how many there were, but if I didn't know any better, which I didn't, I would have thought they were some kind of a SWAT team, but their clothes were peculiar. They had an insignia of an 'L' on their arms and the whole outfit was black and red and made out of a mix of what seemed to be leather and some sort of carbon fibre. They held small black objects that could have been guns, but before I could catch any more details, the time traveler had me by the collar this time.

"Freeze right where you stand!" One of them shouted.

As if his boots were made to break glass Zee shoved one through my back sliding door like a battering ram, his foot shattering the glass. The intruders cocked their black objects, now I was sure they were some kind of gun. The sound forced me back into reality, forgetting about the crazy time talk and Noelle. I didn't need any more coaxing. My blood pumped furiously and adrenaline raced through my entire body as I sprinted away from the pandemonium following the future man through the back door.

The buildings in my neighbourhood were so haphazardly strewn around and close together that outside my back door was a labyrinth of alleys. Only a local could really navigate the maze and even though I had only lived there for six months, I figured it would be our best bet. My muscles tensed as I bolted past my future self taking the lead. We wove our way in and out through the complex network of brick buildings and crumpling concrete, running until we couldn't run any more. We found a narrow corner and squeezed into it. It offered some coverage behind some old smelly bins. Thankfully we couldn't hear any heels in pursuit.

Sweat began to run down my face and my chest heaved as the man slapped a leather band on my wrist, the same as his, and shoved his backpack in my arms.

"Well, that was way too close for comfort wouldn't you say? Okay Charlie, here we go, this is going to be one hell of a ride for you. Hold on to that bag like your life depends on it, because it does. It's going to be 1969 for you shortly and I need you to meet my friend at the Three Greyhounds Pub in Soho," he instructed between breaths.

"Wait, wha? But, how will I know who your friend is?"

"Trust me, when you see him, you'll know."

"I—what?" I stuttered. Without missing another beat, the man gave me a reassuring nod and pressed his thumb hard onto the face of my wristband. All of the sudden, my surroundings shifted. The shape of the world around me twisted into a swirl. All of the colour blended like a kaleidoscope as white flashes glinted in random succession. My feet were no longer on the ground as I fell through a bizarre vortex. The sound was so intense, I couldn't hear my own thoughts—which was probably a good thing since they definitely weren't something you'd want to repeat to your mother.

TWO

AD 2775 - July 18 - Zee

Some might say I let myself get caught. Well, in some ways that would be correct. But I believe was a necessary evil which had to be done in order to keep advancing in my missions - even though I hadn't fully figured out what exactly that mission was. Let's just say I've got myself out of plenty of sticky situations in the last couple of millennia, what was one more? In those times I mostly had full access to my kronometer and all of my other trusted gadgets. But, what would a man's worth be if he didn't challenge himself from time to time?

LINGER had their grubby hands on me at the end of me and my other me's footrace. After snatching and cuffing me up, they brought me back to the year 2775. Ah, this place is really starting to feel like home sweet home. How I've missed the shady organisation I used to dedicate all of my time to. I spent most of my waking and occasional sleeping hours working for The Logistics of Interplanetary

Nucleosynthesis and General Elemental Research company and they really did have a knack of coming up with the most absurd names for everything. I was escorted back to the base which was built into the side of a hill in Sevenoaks and was one of the only places in the southeast of England that wasn't underwater in 2775. They gave me a splendid little room. It had four stone walls at a perfect 90 degree angle each. No windows of course, a couple of chairs, one of which had wrist restraints attached to the arms, this chair was mine, and a large round hapto-holographic table. Hapto-holograms were essentially holograms that would interact with the physical world and therefore they could be used as physical tools, furniture and even sometimes complete buildings. These were commonplace in this time, though no for me, I wasn't allowed to have access to sharp edges which could be hazardous.

"You can wipe that smug look off of your face!" The guard clocked me on the head with the butt of his firearm. Pain radiated through my skull. I tucked my chin against my chest.

"Ow! I want my lawyer!" I mocked loudly, preparing for another blow, but before one came, the door gave a loud click as the bolt withdrew from the lock. Colonel Fairservice came through the door. The Colonel was one of those smug types whom you both hated and admired at the same time. The guard stood to attention with haste.

"Oh hey Colonel Fairservice," I said, pretending and failing to be pleased to see the narcissistic imbecile. Colonel Fairservice was originally the person I used to report to directly while I was working for LINGER though he spent most of his time smoking cigars and reminiscing about how skilful he used to be at Call of Duty XXI - 3rd Remaster - 11th edition 2.

"Now, now, Cortes, none of that will be necessary just yet," Fairservice waved the guard off. The Colonel wore pretty much the same attire as the other members of LINGER, except he had a fancy holographic sash which was decorated in all kinds of glimmering badges and the occasional propaganda advert. Though I would say, this guy honestly has nothing on me. If I had a fancy badge every time I accomplished some great feat, I do believe that I would look like a disco ball.

"Zee is not our enemy, Cortes. Just a fellow worker who has lost his way, again." The Colonel took the seat opposite me while the guard hurried to stand by his side.

"Well, that's a very strange way to say *prisoner*." I sat at an awkward angle with my hands cuffed to the arms of the chair, but I still made eye contact with the man.

"You are not a prisoner." Fairservice said calmly.

"Oh really? That's great news, it's always a good feeling when you think you are in some kind of trouble. But actually, you're completely free to go. Could you please get these cuffs off and give me back my kronometer and I'll be on my way then." The sarcasm was thick in my voice.

"*Your* kronometer?" The Colonel gave a dry laugh, "It's fairly common knowledge around here that you stole that little piece of tech from *us*, and more than one at that. Zee my old friend, you won't be traveling again any time soon, I'm afraid. But, don't worry you won't need to. We just want to know what you've been up to, meddling with time and whatnot without any clearance to do so. Once we've determined your intent, we will begin your rehabilitation process. However, we can indeed get those cuffs off."

Fairservice motioned to Cortes who just stood there, unresponsive. Fairservice cleared his throat and the guard jumped, stumbled, then made his way over to me, unlocking my cuffs.

I pursed my lips in thought for a moment before asking, "Where's General Marriot? Why aren't we at the Moon Base? I figured if LINGER was that worried about what I was up to, they'd send in the big wigs from HQ and isolate me up there with them."

"The moon is much too busy these days, and it would be far too expensive to keep taking you there every single time we find you." Fairservice swiped his hand across the table, brushing away some invisible holographic dust. Something wasn't right. This man was acting way too level headed to be the Colonel Fairservice I know.

"I think you'll find you've only caught me the one ti—"

Then, just like clockwork, the bolt cracked loud again. Another Colonel franticly kicked open the door, this time its Colonel Fone. I jumped in surprise. Colonel Fone was pretty much a Carbon copy of Colonel Fairservice, except Colonel Fone was extremely bad tempered and had an absolutely terrible memory.

"How *dare* you question the command of LINGER!" Fone howled, spit flew from his lips. His face was red as he approached me. I got ready to defend myself, before Fairservice interjected.

"Hey hey, Colonel Fone! It is not your turn yet! I'm only just getting started with the rebellious little rodent" Fairservice sprang from his chair.

"Well, I can't just sit around with this arrogant bastard calling us *incompetent*." Fone turned his attention to the other Colonel.

"Colonel Fone, he didn't call us *incompetent*." Fairservice said, remaining relatively calm.

"No, I certainly did not. I might have only just strongly implied it," I had my hands up in surrender with a small grin on my face, still sitting in the chair.

Fairservice rolled his eyes at me then turned back to Fone, "This is ridiculous Colonel, you know. This really isn't how you play the old good cop bad cop game!"

"I would say that you obviously don't know how to play then do you Colonel Fairservice! Why on earth did you take his cuffs off?" Fone asked, pointing a fat finger in my direction. Cortes jumped again, realising that was his cue. However, his footing wobbled as he fumbled with the cuffs, lost his balance and stumbled to the ground. I had to stifle a laugh. Now I was beginning to understand. Fairservice wasn't cool headed, he was just someone who was a little out of his depth and a little stupid, as indeed was Colonel Fone, it seemed.

LINGER agents were mostly immortal, yes. They had to take their life serum every 200 years or so to stay immortal.

The serum's effect is limited, so a new shot is needed every few hundred years or so to keep the immortality thing going. The serum basically updates the body's cells so that they stop replicating and dying and just replicate, I think. The one drawback with taking any amount of the serum, is that it will make you immediately infertile, so none of those goons have any children. You would have *thought* that this would likely help to improve cognitive ability too. However, these LINGER agents often forgot to sleep, drink, eat or even brush their teeth, leaving their bodies confused and dysfunctional the majority of the time. They were plagued with mood swings, poor cognition, forgetfulness and terrible bad breath.

"While he may seem to be dangerous to you Colonel Fone, he is most certainly not to me, so while I interrogate, the cuffs are off." Fairservice said sternly.

I stared at both men and wondered what they were playing at. They seemed to believe getting me here is going to help me see the greater good of what they are working for. The problem they seemed to not have realised is, I've seen what they think is the greater good and the nonsense they've been fed and made to propagate as the truth, the reality is worse than they can imagine. I'm sure they can comprehend it, it's almost as if they have, but are choosing to ignore the facts. I stared at the wide-open door, thinking of a way to get out of there without being caught. I may have been a little out of it on our way in, but I knew for certain that this place was crawling with armed guards. It was unlike the men in the room to show up somewhere without at least, a battalion.

"Now! Zee! What did you tell that other annoying self of yours? Did you send him somewhere? Did you give him a Kronometer?" Fone's eyes bulged at me, "Please be quick with your answers, we are growing increasingly tired of chasing you around all this time."

"I have no idea what you're talking about," I said. Fone seethed. However, I think my luck was starting to run out. Colonel Fone motioned to Cortes and within seconds my wrists were locked up once more. Fairservice slowly walked over and closed and bolted the door again. Then the three agents all took a place at the round table in front of me.

Fone cocked his head towards the third agent, "Cortes—"

Cortes' eyes jolted towards Colonel Fone as the realisation dawned on him, he quickly jumped up from his chair and shuffled himself backwards towards the door.

"Zee, I get it," Fairservice said in a low voice before

sighing. "I know how hard it is for you what with Winston's death and all. I'm sure it hasn't been easy for you and you feel like the world is falling apart quicker than you can figure out a way to make it all stop."

I balled my fists and clenched my jaw. It took great effort on my part to not throw myself at him and punch him straight in the face. I knew that the repercussions of those actions would probably end up with a lifetime locked up in some cell in the depths of this shit hole. That would just be Winston dying in vain and I just can't have that happen.

"You know nothing."

"I agree, I may not understand what it is like to lose a mentor, but be that as it may, Winston was the worst kind of traitor to our cause, and the higher ups are having reasons to believe that you're about to follow in his footsteps. Now, as someone who was once your superior, I can't have them thinking you're on your way to becoming a traitor when the actual truth is, you're unable to handle the pain of losing someone who was dear to you. So like I said, I get it."

If I wasn't investing all my energy in trying not to punch Colonel Fairservice, or being physically attached to a chair, I might have considered a small round of applause, for that was one hell of a speech, though it wasn't particularly close to any kind of truth. Winston was not a traitor, I knew that just as much as they did, but they were hell bent on labelling him as one because it justified his killing in their minds. I reeled myself back in and maintained my composure. I needed them to think I was on their side with this. I needed them to think that I too thought Winston was a traitor.

"I just find it so hard to believe he'd do something like that," I say finally and look down on the table. To further strengthen my point, I unclenched my fists as a sign to try and show these two that my anger had subsided and I was offering surrender and defeat.

Fone scoffed.

Between the two of them, Colonel Fairservice was fairly convinced that I was forever an ally of LINGER, while Fone clearly believed I was destined to betray and dedicate my entire life to preventing them from accomplishing any of their goals, just like Winston tried to do. Fairservice, despite his unhingedness, seemed, for the most part, to be on my side - whether he realised it or not. He provided me with an excuse for why I stole the kronometers and more importantly, why I was time travelling like it was no one's business. If he thought I'm behaving like this because of Winston's death and not because I wanted to finish what Winston started, I wasn't going to claim otherwise.

"I have a question," Fairservice said and I gave him all my attention. "Why did you bring your past self into this?"

I held his gaze before slowly nodding my head once, and then again. I suppose that question was bound to come up anyway. I sighed to make it look like the question was going to take more than the answer from me. I wondered if I should make my voice quiver, ride longer on the wave of acting out so they understood it was all because of Winston's death.

"I wanted to help myself prepare for what happened, or is going to happen to Winston."

"OK, Elaborate."

"I felt that if my past self was made aware of what happened to Winston, and even got to know him a little bit, then I would be able to pay extra attention to what Winston was thinking and find out if he always had the idea to try and betray LINGER, or if it was just a thought that entered his mind at some point and stuck with him ever since. I was going to try and get my other self to play a little dumb, and see what Winston's excuse for trying to ruin the FTL mission was. You see?"

"FTL?" Fairservice asked, quizzically.

"FTL — Faster Than Light." I said thinking he must be trying to trick me here or something.

"Ah, you must mean the SMFTTSOL drives then?"

I rolled my eyes at the Colonel, "No, I mean the FTL drives. What on this earth is an SMFTTPOL drive?"

Fone's voice cut in, "The So Much Faster Than the Speed of Light Drives. Ha! And you call us incompetent!"

"Colonel Fone, once again, I did not call you incompetent and I know what they are." I said smugly, "I actually just really wanted to hear you say that ridiculous name to me again".

Colonel Fone stood abruptly and looked at me with rage in his eyes. "If you continue to mock this organisation, I will have you locked up in the base for an eternity and force you to listen to 'Ob-La-Di — Ob-La-Da,' for even longer!"

It took my brain a few moments to order the grin off my face, "Ok ok, but in all seriousness though, why not just call them the FTL drives? Faster than Light, or LSD? Light Speed Drives. Actually, maybe that last one will suit you guys better. I always thought that the whole point of shortening a name was for it to actually be short."

"I am fed up with your impudence," Fone barked. "I have just one question for you. If you claim to be on LINGER's side unlike your traitorous and dead mentor, you won't mind answering this question."

It took great effort to shrug. "Yeah, ask me anything."

"Before we take you to meet the Director. Where *exactly* did you send your other self?"

THREE

AD 1969 - April 2 - Charlie

Thankfully it wasn't too long before I felt the ground beneath my feet again, my weight momentarily buckled my knees. My breath caught as I fell forwards slightly into a dark alley. What the hell was that? It was like some crazy super-real hallucination. Surely, I had to be dreaming, right? As I slowly gathered my thoughts I realised that it was night time now, but I could hear people all about the streets. I pulled the pack that Zee gave me over my still shaky shoulder and made my way to the pale glow of street lights that led me out of the alley .

I could hear Zee's words still whizzing through my mind — *It's going to be 1969 for you shortly and I need you to meet my friend at the Three Greyhounds Pub in Soho.* Naturally my instinct was to find out exactly where and when I was, but the thought of this actually being real sent terror through my body. Peeking out of the alley I could see that this certainly did look and smell a lot like the Soho I know, but it was bustling even more than the usual nightlife. There were lines of '65 Austin Morrises, Ford Anglias, and some others I wasn't sure of the name off the top of my head. They even had classic police cars roving around. My god, this is real. Zee was telling the truth, and the bastard has sent me back to 1969! I quickly swivelled myself back into the alleyway and pinned my back against the wall. Calm down Charlie—stay calm—breathe. It felt like hours before I felt brave enough to leave the safety of the only place I can call home in 1969, my alleyway. I liked it here but I just couldn't stay here for the rest of time, whatever that meant now anyway. I had to get a move on, so with my brave face on I slowly edged out into the 60s London streets.

There were a lot of men dressed in suits, women in old style dresses and skirts. There was also an abundance of nylons and heels, topped off with short curled hair. I felt a pit in my stomach as I began to remember what Zee had said to me before my hallucination.

When you see him, you'll know, it's going to be 1969, Three Greyhounds Pub.

My stomach knotted as his words started to make more and more sense with my surroundings. I sucked in a breath as I made my way through the people. I passed a newsagent, pausing just long enough to get a glimpse of the date from a copy of The Guardian. I swallowed hard as the sight etched itself into my brain. *April 2nd 1969*. It wasn't just The Guardian, it was every single newspaper I could see. April 19-freaking-69. I halted at the sight. My muscles refused to move any more, I felt my vision start to blur.

"Geez Louis, watch it will ya mate!" some teenage kid shoved his way past me, but it didn't bother me like it usually would have because, well I wasn't at home now was I? My discombobulation escalated as I pressed myself onto the brick wall of what looked to be a coffee shop. I breathed in the pungent aroma of espresso and stale cigarettes as patrons lulled and laughed on the inside. I steadied my breathing trying my best to stave off the inevitable mental break down I was surely about to have. I cautiously studied the watch—er, the kronometer—that Zee had given me. Obviously, I might be going completely insane, but I quickly and most terrifyingly realised that I was actually perfectly sane and that it actually had sent me back in time.

There was a sudden thud in my chest as adrenaline took me. If this was true, I needed to find whoever Zee needed me to find, and fast. I only wished I had some kind of a description of said person rather than 'if you see him, you'll know'. How will I know? A part of me considered the frightening possibility of the person I'm meeting here being some other version of myself. Was I Stuck here? I really didn't want to be stuck in a foreign millennia for the rest of my days. I had a slightly panicked spring in my step as I stopped to ask anyone I could where this Three Greyhounds Pub might be. Most people I asked had never heard of the place, which obviously only added to my inner terror. But finally, to my relief, a young couple happily pointed me in the right direction. I thanked them overly profusely and made my in the direction they had pointed.

Within about three of minutes extremely fast walking, I came across an old looking building that looked like it had been built hundreds of years ago. Thankfully it was called *The Three Greyhounds*. Having now found this place I'm supposed to be in, I now found myself standing outside it shaking with fear of what might be waiting for me in the inside. I slowly pushed the big wooden door and made my way in. It was full of rowdy customers causing their own little raucous here and there. How the hell am I supposed to know what I'm looking for here? Does this person know I'm coming? Am I looking for a man or a woman? I had so many questions flowing through my mind it only enhanced my desperation to find this person somehow. I scanned the people sitting around the pub's few tables and no-one stood out to me. No-one even noticed my presence. I then turned my attention to the bar area.

I found him almost immediately. He was sitting in the corner of the bar looking directly at me. His winter-white hair was half covering his bright piercingly blue eyes. He wore a long brown leather jacket that looked like it had never been removed. If I was going to be completely honest with you, he just looked kind of tired, like he had seen it all and it had nothing to offer him. As I approached him through the crowd his features became clearer. Dark circles hung beneath his eyes and his stubble darkened his chin. His eyes flickered up and met mine, suddenly he looked as if he was brought back to reality.

"And...Yup, there's that pebble," he said to himself, I assume, as I took a seat next to him.

"Uh, pebble?" I said, sounding unsure of myself. He stared at me for what seemed like minutes, but was probably no more than just a few seconds.

"Now, I'm just gonna throw out a guess here. This is your first time jump kid?" the tired man slugged the rest of his cloudy beer slowly and lazily.

An irritation prickled in my chest. "If by that you mean is it my first time being thrown from my world to a completely different one via time-bending-nightmare-vortex-watch-machine while being chased by space men with guns alongside my identical twin, then yes. Yes, it's my first time."

The look in his eyes went from being just tired to having a hint of sadness in them. "So you met Zee huh? And he sent you here to find me?"

I stared at him and wondered if he is some kind of other, older version of me. I mean I could see all the ways he couldn't be me, but there was something familiar about him. Something that my desperation to understand was hiding from me.

"Name's Winston," he said quietly while resting is empty glass carefully back on the bar.

"Charlie." Realising immediately that he knew exactly who I was.

"Ya, Charlie, gotta say man, not heard that name for quite some time." He nodded his head a smile creeped onto his face. The smile didn't quite reach his eyes as if there was something more than the fact that I made it here. Something my presence in the pub represented.

"You don't look too happy to see me."

"Trust me, I am joyous over your presence. I'm just tired from all the time travelling and having my plan fail every single time. That, and you being here means I'm dead in the future."

"Dead?"

"Zee didn't mention that huh? '69 isn't just a place for us to meet. If all went well, there was absolutely no need for you to be here. We'd meet I'm sure, but more likely in a different timeline. Since you're here with me now, it means I'm dead and our plan has failed. Again, I'm going to go ahead and assume that LINGER has Zee now."

"I—I'm not sure, the last thing I remember was having myself sent through the vortex of doom by my other me, while being chased my psychos with future weapons. I don't know what happened to him after that". I blinked once and tried to take in and process the new information I was getting. I just didn't know how to react to it. Winston was dead. I may not have known the man for a long time, to be honest, I haven't even known him for more than an hour, but there was a sadness in me that I couldn't explain.

"Trust me man, they have him now. Anyway, I don't want to make things any more confusing for you than they already are hey. I'm supposed to make things clearer for you since Zee obviously didn't have enough time to do it. You want something to drink?" The tired Zee asked as he gestured to the barman, "This round's on me. I'm sure you're in need of a drink right about now eh. Oh, speaking of substances, he did give you a dose of the serum before your jump, right?"

I gazed at the man with incredulous eyes, "Yes, I do need a drink right about now. Thank you. Very generous of you," I paused, "but I didn't get a dose of any serum."

"Really? Oof, that's reckless and extremely dangerous. You're lucky that vortex didn't eat you alive," he grimaced before laughing again.

"I'm so glad you think this is funny," my cheeks turned hot.

"Kid, when you get to my age, if you can't find humour in every situation, then you might as well be a dead man." Winston ordered two cloudy looking beers and offered one to me. I took it with a sigh. The man wasn't wrong, I guess. I decided to make myself comfortable, figuring he had a lot of explaining to do. I drank tentatively as I gave him my full attention.

"Your nightmare devil watch is actually called a kronometer. It allows you to travel through time. Two jumps per charge, so right now you have one jump left before you have to charge it again. It's solar powered, so you just have to raise it like a less-fickle plant." He paused at this as he scratched his head with a chuckle. "But that is neither here nor there really. The fact is this, sometime in the future you start working for a very power-hungry corporation called LINGER"

"Yeah! That's who was chasing us, I think," I said as my lips still touched my glass.

"Absolutely it was, and they won't stop chasing you either. If you want the absolute whole truth about what is really going on here, I just don't have it in me anymore. I've been at odds with these people for a very, very, *very* long while. I've spent the better half of my life hopping through time trying to prevent or correct the actions of LINGER, all while trying to avoid them as well."

I studied the man for a moment before asking, "Winston, I have a lot of questions, but I'll throw two at you for now. One, why did you call me a pebble earlier? And two, why is it our job to stop LINGER? Shouldn't there be some super awesome space future police force for this?"

"Ah, well..." the tired man scratched his stubbly chin, "in this line of work, if you ever feel a pebble in your shoe it could mean a handful of things. The most common thing is that, well, you've accidentally got a pebble in your shoe. But the other reason is because a jumper has entered your timeline or they have changed your timeline, yours directly. One appeared in my shoe earlier so I knew I was going to meet you soon."

"That seems a bit, um, random?" I couldn't help but smile at the ridiculous things he was saying.

"I guess it does, the universe has a strange sense of humour let me tell you." He smiled and shook his head like he still was unable to believe his eyes. "You have no idea how great it is to see you like this. It's like a refreshing memory of the first time we met. You look well Charlie. Anyway, LINGER is spending quite a lot of its time chasing after me because in 2749, I stole a copious amount of immortality serum and a handful of kronometers. I needed answers for myself away from prying eyes," the man rubbed his thumb on his glass for a moment in thought, "I stole a lot actually. They would send agents across time scouting for certain minerals and resources for their research into building a machine that could send a human craft faster than the speed of light, though the jury is very much out as to the real reason they are trying to hard to acquire these materials. We would jump back in time, spend a few weeks, sometimes longer, to either find or research the whereabouts of these materials, then return to back our time to charge the devices. One day I was assigned a mission to 1993..."

I raised my brows to question the trail off. He looked at me like he was expecting the year to mean something to me, or he wanted me to remember the rest of the story. I had no idea if I was supposed to have been present on this mission, but the look was starting to make it look like I was, or at least had some kind of involvement with it.

"What happened in 1993? Was I on the mission too?"

Winston quickly shook his head. "No, Charlie, you weren't on the mission. The mission was to go back to the year 1993 in a place called Bilsthorpe, England. It was deemed a possibility that there was a substantial amount of terbimanium at this location. We needed access to it under the guise of being rescue services. So the mission was to cause an *accident* in the mine so we could go in and complete our mission. This was the first time I really knew that LINGER were a genuinely evil organisation and I refused the mission. Needless to say, the mission went ahead anyway with somebody else assigned to it and it was carried with deadly precision. There is nothing I could do to stop it Charlie. I have honestly tried so many times, but it is impossible." He paused for a moment. "There are casualties."

I nodded like it was no big deal. Mining accidents didn't occur often in '93. I think there was only one that made the news, and that was the one – I looked at him with wide eyes hoping he'd see the look in my eyes and tell me it wasn't what I was thinking.

Winston nodded his head and I shook mine. It couldn't be. I just couldn't accept it. My stomach became a pile of knots and I was aware of my breath coming out in heaves. The room seemed to shrink and all my efforts to calm myself went wasted. It didn't make sense.

"The same 1993 accident where my dad—" I started but was unable to finish the sentence.

He nodded his head and offered me a small smile. "The very one your dad died in. Trust me Charlie, I tried to save him, but all my efforts were in vain."

I let my mind work around this new information. "So, you're saying it wasn't an accident at all? My dad was murdered?" I could feel the rage growing inside me.

"It was not an accident Charlie. It was LINGER's doing. They've killed thousands, if not more," he said with a solemn tone, "which is why it became my personal business. The police force of the future is unreliable, incompetent at best. They're also in bed with all the big corporations, especially LINGER"

I grimaced, LINGER was so power hungry that they went around and murdered people all over the world and in different timelines. I began to wonder how many other accidents had not been an *accidental* at all.

"Winston, Why did you try so many times to save my dad?"

Winston looked down at his hands and shook his head, "You and I are close Charlie, we are like family. By that token, your father may as well be my father. But we must move past this and continue with the present - I've already hatched a plan to rescue Zee from whatever cell they have him in this time. You two will need each other through the rest of the journey you have ahead of you."

When he looked up again, he pointed at the bag I was

carrying. "May I?"

I looked at the bag and back at Winston, "uh, sure."

He unzipped my bag and shoved in several small medical looking boxes.

"Listen carefully now Charlie. This is pretty much all the serum I have left, you'll need it for time jumping. Quite how you survived your journey here is a miracle. Anyway, you will need take a dose every 200 years or so. You will know when its time to take a dose, so whatever you do, do not lose this serum. I would suggest you take some right now as you're going on a jump" he said.

I went wide eyed again, "wha—I'm jumping already?"

"Only If you're willing to." Winston held out a small gun-looking device that was made out of some kind of chrome, "Shoot yourself with this in the forearm to take the serum. One vial per dose." He handed me the serum gun.

"In your own time Charlie."

I stared at it for a moment before thinking, thinking nothing at all. I mean what choice did I have here? I can't get back home if I don't. It was right at this point I realised I was part of this now. I had to help Zee stop LINGER somehow.

I held the serum gun against my forearm, closed my eyes and squeezed. —THWIP— It stung like a bee, but besides that, I felt fine. Nothing seemed to change. The serum disappeared into my arm in less than a second. I looked up at Winston.

"OK, there, it's done. Are there likely to be any side effects of this at all?"

Winston looked up at me with a smile. "Charlie, I'm proud of you. Congratulations on being immortal!"

"Are there any side effects Winston?" I was beginning to think he was hiding something about this stuff.

"Yes"

"Yes? Yes what? What are they?"

"Well, the immortality serum makes one sterile. So, if you're not big on having children, then I guess that's not going to be a problem. If you are, it's going to be a bit of an issue."

He waited for me to say if it was going to be a problem, but I said nothing. To be honest, I haven't thought that far ahead in my life. The only part I felt sure of before Zee showed up and played God in my life, was ending up with Noelle.

"Ok Charlie, your mission from me," Winston continued, "is to go back to BC 399. It'll be in Athens. I hope you're a big fan of Socrates as he'll be thrilled to see you, I think."

"Excuse me, did you just say Socrates?"

The man smiled and nodded. I felt a small jolt of excitement immediately followed by absolute terror. Maybe, even if this was just a dream, I could still have some fun with this.

Winston pulled my wrist towards him, clicked on my kronometer and showed me how to punch in the year and prepare for a jump. Amongst a few other bits of information, he typed in BC 399.

"Wait, didn't you say something about this thing needing to charge, how long will that take?" I asked before pushing the down on the screen.

"Oh, well, I think it could be like — thirty years or something or another, depending on the weather of course." The man mumbled.

"Thirty yea—?!" Panic raised in my voice, but it was too late.

With a devilish smile he said, "One more thing Charlie, you can't change the past, no matter how hard you try.

Trust me...I've tried."

He winked and pushed the jump button for me.

FOUR

BC 399 - August 8 - Charlie

Once again, I was slurped up and spat back out by the mind-bending vortex. I found my footing with relative ease, but my head was throbbing and I couldn't seem to see anything. Even so, I could hear the bemused laugh of what sounded like an old man. My vision snapped back as I assessed my surroundings, and the reason for me not being able to see anything was because, it was dark. Only an inadequate sliver of sunlight shone through a tiny opening that was on the upper side of a solid stone wall. There were three of these walls around me and a row of thick metal bars at the far side. Wait, was I in a prison?

"Glad to have you back my boy!" There was the old man, he was in this prison with me. He was balding with a gigantic white fluffy beard. He wore dirty linen wrapped around his waist, while the rest of him was bare. It took me a moment to process what was happening.

"Wh— er, have me back?" I tried not to stumble on my words and failed.

"Zeus in the heavens my boy, do you not recall? I thought I'd have a go at pushing a very appealing button on your armband thingy. I wondered what would happen if I meddled with that device. It seems by the grace of the mighty Apollo himself that it has transported you from here" he gestured toward a space next to him, "to there!" Pointing to where I was standing.

"What? No, I don't think I was ever here and how on earth am I understanding your words? As far as I am aware, I don't speak ancient Greek," I replied, adjusting my backpack.

"*Ancient* Greek? Ho-ho! I do quite love your mannerisms young lad. You've already been over this with me, that was one of my first questions for you when you told me your quite inconceivable story. You said there was a clever little device that you carried on your person that *talked* to your armband. Now what was the name of it again… ah, I think you called it your voxer."

I tapped my chin for a moment, the words of Zee dashed through my mind. That's right, he said something about a device like that. I gave the man a nod.

"I suppose that's right," I said.

The old mans' brows slowly raised with the realisation of what had just happened. "My boy, I do believe that you really aren't the same as you were before, yet as strange as it may seem I sense you are the same, except different and therefore I must deduce that I do not believe we've met before. My name is—"

"Socrates," I finished his sentence, "yeah, you're kind of famous for all of eternity."

"Oh, yes, that's right, your friend did say this to me also, I have to say I just can't seem to wrap my head around the famous for all eternity part," the man chuckled.

"So, what are we imprisoned for today?" I asked.

"We? Oh no, we aren't imprisoned, I am imprisoned. You on the other hand decide to just keep showing up in my cell. Quite the wonderful surprise I must say."

The way his mouth pronounced the words made me realise that he wasn't speaking English like I thought. His mouth movements didn't coincide with the words that came out of them. The voxer, it seemed, only translated his words to English while he spoke Greek, I guessed it translated my English back to ancient Greek. Zee really didn't do enough justice to the work of the voxer.

"That's uhh," I cleared my throat unsure of how to go on. I decided to shift the discussion to him, "What are you in here for?"

"Drunk and disorderly," the man said nonchalantly, taking a seat on a petite wooden bench and picking at his fingernails.

"Er, come again? Is that a joke?" I raised a brow at him. Wasn't this guy a philosopher? Shouldn't he be enlightening me or something?

"Well, that's a half truth I'll admit, although I *was* drunk and very disorderly. However, *they* say I've failed the gods and corrupted the youth, having merely taught them to ask questions. Is it corruption to seek knowledge? Or do the corrupt simply fear being caught?" Socrates gave another chuckle and scratched his beard. Just as I was going to take a seat on the bench opposite the philosopher, my ears picked up with the sound of footsteps, a lot of footsteps. A group of around twelve college-aged young men soon appeared, escorted by a guard. The guard, who was holding a purse full of coins, motioned the group towards our cell.

As the group of men shuffled forwards towards the bars,

my presence inside the cell appeared to catch the guard's attention. He looked straight at me as if trying to see or unsee me, my guess being the later.

"And just who are you supposed to be? How did you get inside this cell?" he asked, stepping closer to the cell.

"Does it matter?" Socrates asked with a small frown on his face. "Why should who he is matter to you, when I am the only subject in question? This boy is doing no harm."

The guard seemed to consider the question. He was clearly about to say something to the contrary, but seemed to reconsider. He turned, and stood to the side still clutching his large purse full of coins.

When the guard had moved, the boys hurried over to the cell, their faces beaming at the sight of the great Socrates. Some of them even trying to push their heads through the bars - but this wasn't quite working out for them. One of them stood watching Socrates like he was devastated to see him in the situation he found himself in. On the contrary I thought to myself, I had a list of teachers as long as my left leg that I wouldn't mind seeing behind bars. So many in fact, that if they ever found themselves in jail and I was awarded the chance to visit, I'd have a grin on my face the entire time.

"Teacher," the boy mumbled, his broad shoulders pressed into the bars. I could see his beard, similar to Socrates', just a little smaller.

"Oh, Plato is that you? What brings you here this fine day?" Socrates rose to his feet and walked towards the youths. Did he just say Plato? Another philosopher? They were all dressed in white linens. It actually looked like some kind of toga party.

"What do you think? We're here to break you out of course. The court can't just throw you away because you think differently than they do. You are the wisest man in all of Athens." The boy named Plato began, "This guard is a friend of Aletheas, he said he'd help us get you out to safety for, well, a considerable amount of drachmas... but, that's beside the point. The point is we can free you."

Socrates beamed at the kids, "Keep your money, my students, use it to help someone who needs it. I do not need any saving."

The students sucked in their breaths and looked amongst each other. Plato was silent for a moment. "What are you saying?" Plato asked quietly.

"I say, I am a man of virtue and I will obey the court's orders." Socrates didn't sound like he was going to budge on the subject.

It was almost too dark to tell, but Plato's body language and voice made it known that he was severely displeased. "Teacher—you and I both know this is a ridiculous overreach of power. You do know what they're going to do to you after your trial? They're going to use you as an example, they're going to—" the boy couldn't finish.

"Execute me?" Socrates said calmly as heavy silence fell upon the group. My stomach sank for everyone. If Socrates had a chance to escape, why didn't he just take it?

"I'm keeping the money, now hurry up!" the guard spat.

"Guard, your services won't be necessary I'm afraid, you may leave and you may also keep your monies." Socrates waved him away. Socrates turned to his pupils once more. "What kind of man would I be if I ran from my fate? What kind of wisdom would I hold if I feared death? For this, as well as so many other things that I cannot give you the answers to, I must accept my fate with grace and dignity. I'm sure in due course, you all will understand this."

"Please, this can't be how it ends. Please reconsider. We don't know what we would do without you," one of the other students begged, his voice cracking on his words.

"None of that now please. However, as you've already lost your money anyway, maybe you can take my friend Charlie here, he still has many stories to unfold in his life," Socrates motioned towards me. I suddenly felt a pit in my stomach. I had no idea if I was supposed to go with them.

"Absolutely not," another student blurted, shoving his way to the front of the group and looking directly at me, then back at his teacher. He was tall with jet black hair and bright green eyes. Something about him sent shivers down my spine. "We're *not* here for Charlie, we're here for you."

"It's quite all right," I spoke before I could think, "I—I mean, I'm here for a reason too. I'm not sure what the reason is just yet, but I guess its something I'll find out soon enough."

Plato raised his brows at me. "Are you a philosopher also?"

Socrates gave a loud belly laugh at the question as he motioned towards me, "Charlie? No, no, my boy, he's just lost and confused, soon to be rectified I'm quite sure."

Green-eyes stared daggers into me. "I bet he is," he hissed.

"Please, leave us now." Socrates demanded of his students, "I do appreciate the sentiment, but Charlie and I have important discussions."

Plato just stood there for several moments looking hurt, but soon nodded his head and turned to leave while holding his glare at me. The other students followed suit. Do they blame me for this? If Zee was part of their lives here, how would I know their working relationships? Feelings of guilt and fear sank in my stomach, even though it wasn't really my fault at all.

"Y—you know why I'm here?" I asked the philosopher as soon as we were alone again. He sat back on his bench, letting his shoulders slump with a large and lengthy sigh.

"Of course, we've talked about it before. There is something you and your foe are here to collect," Socrates rummaged through his linens, pulling out a folded piece of notebook paper. My skin crawled at the thought of where he may have pulled it from. He unfolded the paper gingerly, gazed at the writing, then shook his head, "I really can't make heads or tails of this script, but you wrote it. You said you finally figured it out, but needed me because apparently, I knew where it was."

The man offered me the paper. I took it between my finger and thumb, somewhat terrified to touch it. I leaned in further, so the small bit of light coming in from the window would illuminate the page and I began to read aloud, "*LINGER needs a semi-solid electropositive metal called terbimanium. It is understood this became extinct in ancient earth. It's used to make faster than light travel possible by making the exposure to deadly particle impacts far less severe. The craft used for FTL travel needs to be coated in terbimanium for this to be possible. The agents may be immortal, but they can't survive being turned into puddles...*"

"Nonsense really," Socrates chuckled, scratching his beard, "But, then again, you've already shown me some rather nonsensical things."

My head snapped up at the realisation. It wasn't nonsense, it was true. They were immortal, and apparently, so was I. I wondered for a moment if I should give Socrates the serum so the courts couldn't make a spectacle of him. After all, he had done nothing wrong. If I told him, would he just laugh and give the same response as he gave his students? Has he already accepted his fate? Is it okay to meddle with time travel to such an extent?

"So... do you know where this terbimanium is?" I desperately needed more information.

"I'll be honest with you Charlie, I still have no idea what terbimanium is or why you need it, but as far as groundbreaking developments go, I would say that Sparta fits the script. They've managed to create a new instrument using some type of metal. I suppose it's actually quite the liquid, but not always a liquid. It drops much like water, into tiny golden shimmering pebbles, hits the ground and scuttles off to find somewhere else to go, leaving no trace at all, really quite spectacular."

"What do they use it for?" I asked.

"As I'm lead to believe, they use it to test a new kind of technology. I did get a chance to see it during a demonstration while I was a soldier out in Sparta actually, really rather incredible. They said they don't have much of the this metal, but for what they do have, they've really outdone themselves. They managed to make a device that one can carry around with them. This device can tell them the direction they're facing based on their orientation. So, even in the dark when you can't see the hills of the East, or the starry night sky is hindered by the clouds above, you will still know you're going east because of this device." Socrates looked like he was telling a fantastical story to a child before bed, his hands whirring here and there.

"So, they made a compass." I said as the realisation hit.

"I can't remember what they call it, but if what you seek

isn't in Sparta, I suppose you'll find someone there who would know where it is. I was telling my students about it one day when Charlie, well the other Charlie anyway, overheard me, that's how we met you see. He was so set on finding this metal that I felt it prudent to withhold the information of its whereabouts from him until such time as we had gained each others trust." The philosopher chuckled. "I thought maybe he was going to start a war over it."

I folded the paper and shoved it in my back pocket. I knew what I had to do, I had to find the terbimanium supply and somehow destroy it before any LINGER agents got to it. I hesitated for a moment before asking. "If the court seeks your death, you wouldn't think twice about questioning their sentencing?"

"Well, I very much believe laws should be adhered to. Though I may not agree with how they came about such a decision, I did know the risks from the beginning." Socrates said sternly.

"What if I told you I could make it impossible for you to die? I have a serum, er, tincture. It makes you live endlessly. You could take the serum and fake your death for the court, or just straight out escape right now with your students. I could really use your guidance in my journey sir, I don't even know where I am right now." I heard a pleading in my voice that would've normally embarrassed me if the stakes weren't so high.

Socrates clapped his hand on his knee, bringing me to silence. "No no, none of that, my boy. What kind of philosopher would I be if I were to use some kind of liquid sorcery to escape death? That would just make all of my teachings quite meaningless. I am only a man, and I do suppose my hubris is still at stake—" the philosopher seemed to have recessed back into his thoughts. After a minute or so he looked up at me and continued, "I have told Plato about the metal you seek. I could trust him with my life, as can you my boy. However, after my sentencing I'm sure he will be stricken with grief, so he may not be a such huge help for you or your journey ahead. You should meet with Plato and fill Hekate in on all the details. Hekate is well traveled and adapts easily to almost any environment. In an odd way, he somewhat reminds me of you."

Hekate. I took a mental note of the name. I wasn't surprised by Socrates' response as I somewhat expected it, but there was a pull in my stomach that wished he'd just take the serum. I wondered for a moment if I should just zap him with it while he slept. An idea I quickly shook off.

"If that's what you really want, I will not speak of it again," I said, feeling defeated.

***

Socrates' sentencing came and went, and to nobody's surprise, the court did in fact wish for the philosopher's death. The man didn't wince or even blink at the news. He carried on as if someone was just having a conversation with him about something mundane like the weather. The date was posted and he was to drink a vile of hemlock in his cell.

Before the day of his death, Plato came to the cell by himself on a couple of occasions to talk with his teacher and to try and plead with him to escape, but much to our dismay, the man always brushed off the idea. Afterwards, they only spoke of the future of democracy and where to go from there. They also spoke of me. Plato had few questions and quite easily believed every word his teacher told him, he certainly did have a blind loyalty to the philosopher. My heart sank when I realised how hard his death would be to Plato.

Judgement Day was upon us, Socrates' students all gathered around as well as all of the politicians. Socrates gave a profound speech defending his teachings and ending by saying how he would have never changed a thing about his life. It wouldn't be a stretch to say that he had the strongest mind of any man I have ever met, albeit a little off his rocker. Some of his students shed tears, but most remained stone-faced, including Plato, who must have prepared himself for this day for a very long time.

Somehow the politicians were not in the least bit swayed by Socrates' speech. I guess that's what greed and power does to men. They will generally opt out of what is right, for what is easy and powerful. Their corruption was threatened by the philosopher, so he had to be taken care of. In a way it reminded me of LINGER, as they too would kill the innocent if it was justified by their greed. A rage burned in my stomach as my look mirrored Plato's. Stone-like and cold.

The poison was offered to the philosopher who took it without falter. He guzzled it down as if it were the finest of wines, handing the goblet back to the guard and smacking his lips. "Mmm, got any more where that came from?" he chuckled, but the joke was lost amongst the crowd. They then ordered him to walk. The man trudged around the cell. He walked and walked until his limbs shook and his breathing became haggard. It probably wasn't that long, but it felt like eternity before his legs gave out and when they did, he tried to crawl. He may have gotten only few feet further until the crawling didn't work either. He was limp, face down in the cell with his breaths heaving, laden with one or two coughing fits. Finally, there was silence, as the rise and fall of his lungs stopped. I didn't avert my gaze. I watched the entire thing and realised that I was holding my breath.

The politicians congratulated themselves before leaving. They allowed us some time alone with his body before they took him away for good. The philosopher was close enough to the bars for his students to reach through and caress his curly white hair. More were crying now as I sat just in the corner biting the inside of my cheek. All I could feel was heat, radiating from my face.

My eyes caught the glare of the green-eyed student from the other day. He was staring directly at me. I would have probably freaked out if I wasn't so caught up in the moment. The boy made his way toward me, leaning down to look at me at eye level. "Plato says you're not as dense as the old man," he whispered so quietly that even I was unsure of what he said.

"Excuse me?" I asked incredulously.

He gave me a smirk. "Stay up tonight, Charlie. Plato and I will be back to get you out of here," and with that, he stood, turned on his heel and vanished down the corridor. My heart was heavy as I looked back at the students saying their farewells to their departed teacher. Plato held my gaze now, giving me a slight nod. I gulped at the realisation. That scary green-eyed kid was Hekate. Fabulous, I could tell that my trip to Sparta was going to be an interesting one.

FIVE

BC 399 - August 9 - Charlie

I clutched on to my bag and sat up against the stone wall of the cell, alone with nobody but my thoughts. I was still struggling to come to terms with what had happened in my life over the past couple of days. It was simply mind-boggling to even try and comprehend what was happening to me. So many questions were swirling around in my mind, it was hard to pin just one of them down to attempt to give it some sort of a reasonable answer. Why me? How many versions of me are there drifting around in time? Was that really Socrates? Why has no-one questioned why I have the words Levis written on my t-shirt and Nike Air written on my shoes? Why couldn't Winston and Zee get to the terbimanium? Would anyone notice I wasn't around anymore after Zee sent me to 1969?

The realisation I simply couldn't answer any of these questions sent sudden wave of dysphoria over me, knowing that there was no-one at home who was going to even notice that I wasn't there. I threaded my fingers into my hair, froze for a second then frantically ruffled it in the distant hope that some sense might magically appear. It was obvious, I badly needed a haircut.

Just as promised, in the quiet hours of the night, Hekate and Plato showed up with the same guard as the first night they appeared, it seemed the stingy guard had decided to help after all. My short time locked up without Socrates the philosopher was the only time of my incarceration that I actually felt like I wasn't behind bars. Though we'd only known each other for a matter of hours, Socrates had a strange way of making you feel free, who would've thought?

My stomach churned at the thought of his demise when the guard knocked me out of my thinking with his raspy voice.

"Well, are you comin' or what?"

I gave the man a curt nod, though I don't know why. It was so dark in the corridor I doubt he could have seen me very well. My shoes scraped over the rough ground as I made my way out, my heart skipped a beat.

Holy crap, I was breaking out of jail—for real! I didn't know whether to feel excited or to feel embarrassed that this was probably one of the most exciting moments of my life so far.

The excitement was all internal though because, leaving the cell was about as thrilling as being discharged from the hospital after passing a particularly painful kidney stone. Not that I know what that feels like.

Hekate quickly wrapped me in some kind of oversized cloak.

"Put this chlamys on and keep it on, you stick out like a sore thumb," he muttered, but I didn't know if he was actually talking to me or just making a painfully obvious observation.

"Take off those trainers." Hekate said, turning his head sideways to check if there was anyone around. I quickly obliged, more or less because I didn't really have much of a choice. When my bare soles hit the cool ground, a pair of leather sandals fell to the floor simultaneously beside them. I didn't need to be told what to do. I strapped them to my feet the best I could. They felt awkward, but I had to make it work. I scooped my trainers under my arm and readjusted my backpack.

Plato and the guard finished speaking in hushed voices before proceeding, Plato leading the way. "This corridor isn't used anymore... we shouldn't run into any problems," Plato said as he passed us by. The guard turned in the opposite direction, I guess he was done here then. We trudged our way through the narrow corridor with only a single flaming torch in the hands of Plato to guide us.

I couldn't tell if my mind was playing tricks on me or not, but I could've sworn I felt my limbs brushing cobwebs as we walked. Plato was in front of me while Hekate took the rear and all of the sudden my nerves began to waver. What if that guard was lying? It did appear that loyalty wasn't his forté, but rather he fancied a purse bloated with coins. What if this was a trap? I gulped at the realisation that we could be ambushed at any moment. I knew that I was technically immortal, but it was only natural. I am human after all, I think. What would happen if the young men helping met their end because of me? I did all I could to dislodge the thought from my head.

"The exit is just up ahead," Plato whispered back to us.

We were able to get out of the Prison surprisingly, without a single hitch. I guess the guard thought that he was indeed paid reasonably enough.

The cool air hit me as I smelt the wildflowers of that

moonless night. It was my first taste of real fresh air in such a long time, I hadn't realised how much I missed it. We used the backroads and the darkness of the night as cover as we made our way out of the agora to Hekate's oikos in Ceramics.

I didn't actually know the names of the districts in Athens at the time, but I was eavesdropping quite heavily whenever the students spoke amongst each other. Hekate said that we would be safe and well-hidden at his place, but I had a niggling feeling that he didn't particularly like me, so I was wary nonetheless.

Hekate's home was a stout square structure made up of wood and clay bricks. It was attached to a potter's workshop at one end and another family's home on the other. It looked sturdy and comfortable in my weary eyes. Hekate pulled open the large wooden doors slowly, trying not to make a sound.

"I don't want to draw any unnecessary attention, so we won't light the lamps tonight," Plato said as we entered the dark house. "It'll be best to get some rest now, for tomorrow will be busy."

I made no protest. Plato and Hekate retired to separate chambers as I found myself making camp on the couch in the main room. They said it was a couch, but it was made out of wood and felt more like a bench. It had an itchy tapestry draped over it. But, I tried to be thankful for what I had, as I pulled the excess tapestry around myself and did my best to get comfortable as another question came roaring into my mind and my nerves squeezed my chest like a hungry python, and I was the prey.

"Did Hekate use the word *trainers*?"

***

I woke up in the early hours of the morning with the bustle of the streets outside. I heard pots clank and people holler greetings to each other as they made their way to the market. I must've been more tired than I thought because I didn't remember falling asleep.

The couch was hard against my back and suddenly, I became glad to be awake, even if it was just to get off of the damn thing. I sat up and stretched, scanning the main room. For some reason, in my head, I always thought of ancient Greece as large and grand with everything cut from marble and stone, but from what I had seen so far, that definitely wasn't the case.

The room's walls had been stained with beige and the floor was nothing more than meticulously packed soil. In a far corner was a pile of hay that I could only assume served as a play space for some kind of farm animal at one point in time, and closer to where I sat was a simple wooden table. Other than the tapestry that hung around my shoulders, there wasn't much decoration anywhere else in the room.

The sun shone through cracks in the large wooden doors and with some noted irony, I felt as if I was in fact still imprisoned. There was no sign of Plato or Hekate yet, so I lugged my small belongings to the table and assessed my gear.

The ground was cold beneath my bare feet. I tapped at the kronometer on my wrist, but to no avail. Like a dead cellphone, it didn't show any signs of life. LINGER's technology was as incredibly amazing as it was devastatingly rubbish, hundreds of years into the future and they still haven't figured out battery life. I clicked my tongue at the thing and checked my pack. I still had the translator, the serum vials, the injector gun, the notebook and pens, and the note that Zee had left with Socrates.

I opened the note once more and knitted my brows at it.

LINGER needed terbimanium in order to travel faster than the speed of light. If their spacecraft wasn't coated in the stuff, it would be exposed to some incredibly nasty rays, and not only would the craft suffer damage, but the pilots and crew would evidently turn into gooey puddles of human slush. Their immortality serum lacked the benefit of full body regeneration it seemed. I leaned back in my chair and looked up, stroking my chin briefly. So basically this semi-liquid metal was like a mega sunscreen for spaceships, and it was only in ancient Sparta. I had to find the terbimanium reserve in Sparta and destroy it before any agents showed up, that is, if they weren't there already.

"How'd you sleep?" Hekate asked as he made his way into the room, the sound of his voice making me visibly jump.

"Jesus, you scared the daylights out of me," I held a hand over my chest.

"That's unfortunate, maybe you should try not to think so hard," He replied. He had plates of bread as Plato followed close behind with goblets. They set the breakfast on the table and sat with me, offering me my portion. I took the food gratefully.

The bread was in fact bread, but it was as hard as rock. I

watched as they dipped theirs into their goblets before eating. I followed suit. The wine in the goblet made the bread soft enough to chew and swallow, and it actually tasted rather pleasant. Needless to say, I finished my meal first like a starved orphan. The students shot each other a look before Plato excused himself to fetch me some more breakfast.

"My apologies, you must be starved," Hekate said once Plato disappeared into the kitchen.

I looked up at him and shook my head.

"It's okay, there's enough for everyone." Hekate continued, as he leaned forward, resting his chin on top of his threaded fingers. "So, Charlie, our teacher thought it was more important that you be in the world than himself. Care to enlighten us as to why that is?"

"Well, he…" my stomach sank as I continued, "he heard my story and decided that I needed to see it through. Plus he said he'd never defy the court's sentence anyway."

"I know this to be true. So, what is your story then? Plato and I would love to know the details since we are sticking our necks out for you. Sound like a fair trade?" his bright green eyes never left mine. I bit the inside of my cheek. He did have a point, but something felt odd about the way he questioned, like he knew something and wasn't letting me in on it, could I really trust these two?

"Absolutely, but hey, do you guys have a bathroom? My stomach is in knots," I asked gingerly. "I mean, you know, a latrine?" Hekate smiled at me for the first time, even though it didn't look genuine at all, I suppose it was a start.

"Aphedron," he gestured toward a door in the kitchen. I pulled my pack on my shoulder, thanked him, and made my way towards the door, nearly bumping into Plato as he came back with more bread and wine.

To my amazement, the bathroom almost looked identical to the one back in my flat. Besides the fact that everything was made of clay and stone. But then, there was a tub, a toilet, and even a hand sink. I wasn't sure if this was common in all of the homes, or if Socrates's students were from some kind of wealthy families. Whichever the case, I was just glad for a proper place to wash my face.

Out of nothing more than a pure curiosity, I removed the lid of one of the several baskets on top of the stone counter. I wondered if they used toothbrushes or toothpaste or what else they could've used in ancient times. I gazed into the basket and blinked several times to make sure my eyes weren't deceiving me. I stared at a used disposable razor and a can of shaving cream. My pulse lurched as I made the realisation. Either Gillette is a much older company than I could've ever imagined, or somebody besides myself was here or had been here, or was still here and was from the future. I replaced the lid carefully to make the basket look undisturbed before I made my way back into the main room. The young men had finished their breakfast and were stuffing a bag. I tried to act casual as I sat back at the table to finish my breakfast.

"I need your help getting to Sparta," I said while holding my hand over my kronometer. I wanted to rip it off like a used Band-Aid and not look any more suspicious than I already did to them. After all, I now had a suspicion that one of them was a LINGER agent, or worse, which meant I had the advantage. Or, I suppose that meant we were on equal ground. That being said, It really didn't take a genius to deduce who I was at this point.

"What exactly is it in Sparta, that you and the person who came before you, Zee was his name if I recall correctly, want so badly?" Hekate asked without looking up.

Wait what? Did he just mention Zee or my ears played tricks on me? "Did you just say Zee?"

Hekate looked up before replying. "You know when I saw you at first I thought you were Zee, but with the nervous look on your face and the aura you carried, I was sure you weren't him. Though he told me someone else who looked exactly like him would come. I didn't believe it at first. I thought it was one of his weird jokes, but well, here you are..." He waved his arm in a circular motion.

"Ah, that explains it." But I still had more questions.

"It sounds like you are looking for something important, Charlie. I'm sure my friend here would have no problem showing you the way to Sparta, even though I have to admit, I'm totally lost on what you young gentlemen just said," Plato began, he stood up and offered a weak smile. "I have much to do here in Athens. As you probably already know, my mentor was just wrongly murdered by the court."

His matter-of-fact voice made my heart sink. I hung my head and nodded.

"Of course Plato. I don't have a problem with going alone with Charlie, I love Sparta. The women there are lean and smart, they're actually allowed to leave the house too!" Hekate said with a laugh. "However, I can't just take the gods-know-how-long out of my life to travel all the way to

Sparta for an important reason that is still unknown to me." Hekate looked directly at me. "What is your business in Sparta? How did you get here? Did Zee send you after he disappeared without a single trace? I'm going to need some answers."

I thought for a moment, Zee obviously didn't let him on as to why he came here, therefore he definitely had a reason not to.

Plato seemed to agree with the sentiment, looking back at me inquisitively to hear my response. Fair enough, I thought. I made an extra effort to choose my words carefully. "There is something I am seeking that your late mentor believed to be there. He said he saw it once during a demonstration--"

"The compass demonstration?" Plato interrupted, his arms were crossed. "Why do you seek this?"

"Perhaps to help him find his way back to Athens," Hekate chuckled, securing the pack he was loading. I pursed my lips at him.

Hekate tossed the pack at me without any hesitation. I caught it with a thud. It wasn't as heavy as I was expecting, but it wasn't light either.

"It's for you, sore thumb. We don't need you drawing any unnecessary attention with your… odd clothes, I wonder why Zee didn't prep you on this." Hekate cocked a brow at me.

Before I could reply, Plato cleared his throat. "I see there is clearly sensitively in this subject, but if our mentor believed in you then we shall too. All I ask is that you tell us if this is some scheme that could hurt civilians."

I blinked at the words. Hurt civilians? "Of course I'm not planning on hurting anybody. On the contrary, I'm trying to save lives."

"Well, then, I will let you guys get to it. If there's anything I can assist you with, feel free to let me know before you leave. Though I am very busy, I am more than willing to make time for our teacher's dying wish." Plato's glare wasn't aggressive, but I could still feel the daggers in it. Maybe I was experiencing what they call survivor's guilt.

I hung my head once more. "Of course. Thank you Plato."

***

It took almost a week for Hekate and I to travel to Sparta.

We travelled the entire way on horseback. Riding a horse was something I had to learn to do extremely fast. Thankfully the horses which were owned by Hekate were quite small and barely ever felt like doing anything more than a slow paced trot. We never spoke of our personal lives so I still didn't know what his trade was, but turns out I was correct about Hekate having access to some form of wealth. All I really knew about him was that he was one of the old philosopher's students. Or used to be, I guess. Socrates said he was easily adaptable and knew his way around Greece, so I suppose I should have figured as much.

Ancient traveling was a little different from back in my time. There was lots of camping and lugging, and when I say camping, we didn't have a tent. It was just lying down on an itchy blanket out in the open air. When we were lucky, we could stay the night in a town where we and our horses could get proper rest. I was a little scared of the animal at first, but when I realised they were basically just big dogs, I warmed up rather fast. My horse's name was Kyros, a chestnut coloured animal and he was my favourite part of the journey. It wasn't a stretch to say that he was a better travel companion than the brash Hekate.

It took us two days to get to our first stop, the city of

Argos. There was no need to pay for a room because of course Hekate had friends who lived there. I was doing pretty okay at keeping a low profile, as I clumsily learned the customs and how to not be a socially awkward weirdo. Sometimes, I would say something so ridiculous that Hekate couldn't help but laugh, so I assume that was a good thing. He was a hard egg to crack, but since it seems that he was now in a lighter mood and we had a roof over our heads, I decided to ask more about Zee and his stay in Athens.

"Uhhm, so, can you tell me more about this Zee fellow? I asked, actually not expecting a response from him, but the hope was there."

"Ah Zee, the mysterious Zee," he started with a smile, "I first noticed him speaking to our philosopher after a class. I thought at first he wanted to join in one of our classes, but later on it came to light that he wasn't interested in that at all. He was after something very different. So, one day I decided to corner him, you know, just to try and get answers from this mysterious man who just seemed to show up out of thin air. Anyway, I'd like to say that we almost became friends. I mean, when he wasn't with Socrates he was either at my house or someplace else trying to get answers for his mission I suppose. It turns out that he, like you, was looking for something that obviously had significant importance to him." He sighed and threw his head back, as though to recollect a particular memory. "It was one evening, while Zee and I were having some wine and some fine meats, he told me he might have possibly found the place at which this item might be located, but his time was limited. He told me that there were people chasing after him and warned me that he might have to send someone else to help if he should have to suddenly leave." He lowered his head to look at me. "And here you are," he laughed. "You guys seem quite the opposite though, in a good way." He placed, both his arms at the back of his head and closed his eyes.

I assumed that meant end of discussion.

We spent two nights in Argos, careful not to burn ourselves out with travel. It was a large city with a lot of people. It was the first time in a long time that I felt stress-free. I got along great with Hekate's friends as we drank wine and ate delicious food as I never had before. Our horses stayed at a place that I can only describe as an equestrian spa, while Hekate's friends took us out to the theatre. The streets buzzed with people and music and for a moment I thought that maybe I could just settle here for the remaining years I needed to charge my kronometer. But, all goods things must come to an end. On the third morning, we set off once again.

It took another full days riding before we arrived in a town called Tegea, where we spent another two nights. We did in fact have to pay for a room and stable while there. Hekate had told me that Tegea was the oldest city we were going to visit and that they had very conservative customs. It wasn't going to be like back in Argos, but it was still a nice place to rest. The city was filled with art, but he was right, it was calm and quiet - which I very much appreciated. Although I did quite enjoy the party nights of Argos, it was a much-needed relief to be able to gather myself for a while before making it to our main destination. On the third morning, we set out once more.

It was two more days before we finally arrived at the outskirts of Sparta.

SIX

AD 2775 - July 28 - Zee

Handcuffed once more, I stood looking up in unabridged awe at the Starship. From the outside it didn't appear to be big enough to carry more than one person. Weirdly, it also seemed to be slightly translucent, though I couldn't see anything on the inside. It really was quite magnificent to look at.

I knew from my time working at LINGER that these things were generally called Nimas. I'm not sure why this was the name given to them, though I've never really given it all that much thought, maybe it was a word that just sounded good. They were made from an Iridium and Moscovium alloy which had a relatively high density, they looked matte in colour, but seemed to glow radiantly while bouncing back reflections of even the faintest of light. It really was a masterpiece. The crème de la crème you might say. If I were not on my way to meet sudden death the thought of spending a little bit of time onboard a ship of this caliber might have filled me with a little bit more joy.

"Bring down the stairs Fairservice! We don't have all day" Colonel Fone said while standing just underneath the craft, with irritation dancing all around the words he spoke.

Fairservice, clearly wary of Fone's grumpy tendencies, adhered and the stairs of the craft began to materialise in front of our eyes.

As we began to walk up the silvery glowing stairs, I half expected them to give way as they seemed, well, a little floaty, flimsy and sort of wispy. Inside, there were no visible lights at all, yet it was perfectly lit and absolutely devoid of any type of shadow. It appeared to be at least twenty times larger on the inside than the perceived size from the outside and there was a glass-like dome which sat across the top which felt like some kind of crown on the fastigium of perfection. Conveniently, there happened to be three seats, all circling one smooth centre console with nothing but a few brightly coloured lights or buttons and an indentation in the shape of a human hand. My assumption has always been that once the pilot places his hand into the indentation, the craft inherits that pilots conscious mind and the ship and the pilots consciousness becomes entwined, enabling the pilot to perfectly control the craft with ease. There were also three small boxes under each seat which all contained a tasty stash of sweet goodies. It felt like VIP treatment.

These goons probably wanted me to feel comfortable before meeting the Director. He was the man in charge and a notoriously grumpy fellow whom I pray you don't get to meet if you one day you ever had the misfortune to work at LINGER. Though it has to be said, I've never really spoken to him, even with all my numerous visits to the moon-base. But this time around, it seemed as though I was in extra double trouble.

I took the only seat left as the Colonels obviously each had a favourite seat. Just as if the music had been turned off in a game of musical chairs, they silently scrambled for a seat like two school children desperate for a small prize. Once I was seated, I immediately reached for the goodie box from under the seat and made myself at home.

Colonel Fone and Colonel Fairservice then simultaneously rested their hands into the indentation in front of them, the ship hummed and vibrated, followed by a pleasant sounding female voice "This ship has manual flight mode disabled, please remove your hand from the crenel. Thank you for your cooperation". After a quick glance at each other and then over to me, they calmly removed their hands from the crenel and in unison, let out a wheeze of disappointment.

As I looked up, I could see the sky through the glass dome of the starship turn instantly from a deep blue to black, no stars, just black. We had gone from pretty much ground level to outer space in the blink of an eye and I didn't feel even the slightest hint of motion from in here, truly amazing. Then within another second the dark skies of the universe began to flex its supremacy all around us in whirlpools of colour and sparks of light as we edged closer and closer to the LINGER moon-base.

Three minutes later and I had already eaten half of my goodie stash. Red and green chewy sweets all in the shapes of the moon, basically spherical, very original. I was sure to be needing a nap after all the sugar I had just pumped down my system.

Just as I was fishing the last chew-ball out of its little plastic bag, I felt the ship begin to slow and the colours and lights started to disappear. Looking out into the endless vast space the universe had to offer, I asked the Colonels rhetorically. "Hey, guys. Have you ever wondered whether there really is actually a some kind of supreme being out there, you know, watching over us?"

"Well, I certainly believe there is a God of some kind of—I mean, I cant say whether it's a man, a woman or a thing, or even a nothing. But there is definitely something out there." Fairservice replied confidently.

I couldn't help but give a little laugh. "You believe there is a god who could be a nothing but definitely a something. Got it, makes perfect sense."

Fone glared at me before chipping in. "If there was a something, I mean like a person or something, not a nothing something person or a just a nothing, I'd say he or she isn't doing his or her job properly. I mean look at us, we are pretty much gods ourselves now, we can live for eternity, we have control over almost everything we have discovered and we've been hearing of this second coming of Julius Christ since Jesus Caesar knew how to walk. But where is he till now? I can't help but see it as a just one big giant fib".

"You mean Jesus Christ right?" I said to Colonel Fone raising my index finger cautiously.

"Yes, that's what I said Zee! Careful of your impudence now, might I remind you of the current situation you find yourself in and the powers we have to change the situation are strong. For better or for worse." Fone said, clearly enjoying his moment of power over me.

"Right, whatever you say Colonel, I apologise." I said acrimoniously before continuing. "So would you say our destiny has been written and we can't change it, not matter what we do or even how hard we might try?"

"Haha, of course our destiny can be changed." Fone replied, "I mean, look at the technology we have created over the past 30 years. You know the kind of technology you thought was a great idea to steal from us." He gave me an angry look then returned his face to the front view of the ship. "With that technology, you can go back and change your destiny. Make yourself do things you didn't do at any given period of your life."

"Ok, but what if it's in your destiny to change your destiny?"

It got Fone thinking.

I let out a small chuckle. Life was challenging enough without having to think about theoretical concepts acting as a decoy to sway us from knowing the truth about what it offered.

"Just face it," I continued. "You guys need the comfort of justifying all things that are happening in ways that you can easily understand, a want to imbue events with emotionally charged rhetoric, but the belief of any type of destiny obviously requires a surrender of critical thinking —you guys aren't into surrendering by any chance are you?"

The remaining brain power in Fone's head quickly sparked into action. He swiftly unbuckled his seatbelt, jumped up from his seat and pounced upon me, grabbing my collar and pinning me into my seat. The two oversized hands jerked me closer to his face, so I could smell his breath which was something close to a two day old fish finger sandwich and mud. I pursed my mouth, squeezed my nose and shut my eyes.

"Stop trying to trick us Zee! You don't have the brainpower!" Fone's lips were quivering with rage. I could only remain in place, eyes wide open and mouth firmly shut.

Some awkward seconds later, we were thankfully in view of the moon-base where the promise of getting away from these two was truly an enjoyable thought.

By now, I'd been to the moon-base a few times. In fact,

every time myself and Winston had been captured we wound up here at the moon-base . The sadness of Winston's death still hovered over me. Sure, potentially I could see him whenever I wanted to, but when all this is over, he's really gone, a pain right in the gut.

The LINGER moon-base is absolutely monstrous in size. It always makes me feel a little dizzy as I got closer and closer to it. The sheer size of it is completely overwhelming. Its architectural design is first-rate and it boasts the finest construction materials the discovered universe had to offer and of course, the best of view of the earth you could possibly imagine. The base is in an isolated part of the moon in an attempt to keep it out of the reach of outsiders. Not many dare to come here anyway, due to the obvious harsh conditions inherent to it and the fact that the people who occupy it are notoriously unfriendly.

The base has a very clever way of providing itself with clean breathable air. An idea that I doubt LINGER came up with all by themselves, certainly not the agency as it currently is anyway. Perhaps some decades ago there were some smarter people working for this organisation, perhaps.

The surface of the moon is covered with a fine powdery material called the lunar regolith. This stuff is put into a molten calcium chloride bath before an electrolytic cell is used on it. Passing an electric current through the bath causes the oxygen to be extracted from the regolith and migrate across the salt to be collected at an anode. As a bonus this process also converts the regolith into a usable metal alloy. The results are pure oxygen at the anode side and metal alloys at the other, clever.

As we approached the massive doors of the moon-base, I took one last look up through the glass dome on the Starship. Out there in the black of space was Earth, the stunning blue and white, but fragile oasis in the vastness of space. Looking at the Earth from this perspective had always made me feel so small and at the very same time, it made me feel so powerful. Just being able to see so much of the world that us humans began our journey on.

"Moon to Zee, come in." Fone said in attempting his best impression of a tannoy.

"Wha—I'm in." I said, struggling to remove my gaze from the awesome sight out of the glass dome.

The arrival port of the moon-base opened up in front of us and green flowing lights ushered us into an air lock, then the huge doors closed tightly behind us silently as two more doors then opened up to reveal the inside of LINGER's moon-base. It was vast, there were glass domes littering the whole place, ships flying around inside going from place to place. There was even a giant circular garden with trees, grass and even a few small lakes, that were around the edges of the entire base. The ship automatically made its way slowly through the complex, passing hangers, loading bays, engineering docks and the countless other areas that are needed to keep this gigantic place running.

Finally the ship touched down on pad 23 and the interior of the ship went from a deep blue colour to a pale white as the sparkly floaty stairs formed below us leading to the pad floor. The Colonels beckoned me to go down first so I obliged and made my way slowly down to the deck. I gave a huge stretch as my feet hit solid ground.

It really was one hell of a ride. I made a mental note to try and get a ride on this ship again if I ever made it out of here alive, preferably without these the high ranking baboons as company.

"This way Zee," Fairservice said pointing towards an open passageway ahead of us.

The stench of calcium chloride filled the passage we entered as we made our way towards the Director's office.

"Ah!..." I sighed, taking it in with full breaths. "Calcium Chloride, anyone else enjoy smoking a powdered version of it? Makes you relax and want to fight scary holograms at the same time."

Fone scoffed. "That is ridiculous and probably illegal."

I grinned. "It's only illegal when you are caught Colonel".

"Time travel is illegal, we've caught you doing that so, busted!" Fone said with a grin

"Firstly, you haven't ever actually caught me in the act of time travelling. Secondly I haven't seen the Director yet, so it doubly doesn't count. Also, if I escape, it could simply mean I wasn't even here in the first place. So there..."

Fone fell quiet.

"But I actually want to ask this, if time travel is illegal, why then do you time travel to stop time travel? Do you have some kind of special time travel pass?"

In reality, I was only trying to buy myself some time. And, I really loved playing with their limited intelligence. That little bit of intelligence the serum had left them to keep them from having the actual intelligence of a newborn chimpanzee.

They pondered on the question and we trudged forward. I didn't bother to try and listen to what they were mumbling about. I had other plans.

A ring from Fairservice's communicator came in. We stopped so he could answer the call. I heard some unintelligible chattering from the other side. Fairservice nodded, "okay, we will, yup, okay," he said at various intervals during the call before hanging up the communicator.

"The director is busy right now, so we should probably wait for him in the bar area." Fairservice said raising his eyebrows, clearly pleased at the chance of getting some kind of beverage inside him.

With that, we promptly changed direction and headed down a widening hallway that lead into one of the base's many bars. This particular one was called The *Hidden Stormcloud Hideout*. It was full of workers, civilians, bar staff and the odd soldier dotted about the place. Certainly a busy place to be in and potentially the perfect place to sneak away, hopefully without being noticed.

We found a table in the very centre of the bar area. As Colonel Fone and I took a seat, Fairservice turned around and headed straight for the bar, clearly eager for some beer. He was well known for his penchant for a tipple or two whenever he could get his hands on it. I decided that now was the perfect chance to ask Colonel Fone if he had found an answer to the earlier question I had posed to them.

"So, What's your answer then Colonel?" I asked.

"What answer? Are you testing me again?" Fone asked, presenting his usual confused face.

How shocking, he had forgotten the question.

"You know, the one about the legalities of time travel. Even for agents of LINGER such as yourselves."

Fone went into deep thought, and just as his mouth was about to say something, his finger raised towards me and he got up and headed straight for fairservice over at the bar area. "Uh, I'll be back. Don't move a muscle you." Came his words as he took, presumably to ask Colonel Fone for an answer. I eyed Fone like a hawk as he made his way over to Fairservice and chose my moment.

I held my breath and got up from my chair, swiftly walked around the table and headed in the exact opposite direction to the bar area, casually hiding my face from people. I didn't want to raise any alarm. After all my face has been here many times before and the chances of being recognised were very real. After leaving the bar, I headed down another passageway and came to a door that had the words, *AUTHORISED ACCESS ONLY* on it. I could hear the sounds of clanking metals and clattering of tools on the other side. I slowly pulled the handle. Open! Of course it was. I cautiously and gently pushed the door open and peered in.

"Holy shit!" I couldn't help but say it out loud. Before my very eyes there was something I'd never seen before, three vast, floating and perfectly spherical shiny orbs in the middle of some kind of compact hanger. There were people moving about in oily looking overalls wearing strange holographic helmets, each one seemed assigned to a particular ship. Then it dawned on me. These must be the FTL ships, surely. Have they built them already? Indeed, one of them did look like it might be completed as it was hovering a few feet above the ground and making a humming sound like I'd never heard or experienced before. It was making all my hairs stand on end. I could feel the sound coursing through my entire body, quite enjoyable really.

How on-the-moon have they managed to develop the FTL ships already? I thought they were decades away from any sort of completed ship. I decided to make way to the open plan office over to the side of the hanger. There was someone in mind I wanted to see, even just briefly.

I knocked on the office door and opened it without waiting for an answer. There she was, her short blonde braids still as beautiful ever, her eyes gleaming with brilliance and the little blemishes of a few red spots on her face made her look even prettier. Thin red glasses finished the job and tuned her into an actual angel.

It was Kate. Not the shady, grumpy and totally unapproachable Kate I had worked with in what now seemed like a totally former lifetime. This Kate was the exact opposite, slightly nerdy, utterly beautiful and had a bewitching way about her. I walked up to the front of her desk and rested my arms on it. Her eyes were fixated on the monitor in front of her, she hadn't noticed I was even there.

"Hola Senõrita," I said, attempting to use my best Spanish intonation.

She looked up and her cheeks turned red. "Oh, hey," she had to clear her throat. "Hi Zee", she appeared to be visibly flustered.

"Kate, I can't tell you how hard it is to find this place. Even the Uber driver got himself completely lost." I smirked as I moved around her desk to see what she was working on. Looking over her desk, an object caught my eye. It was a glowing blue cube-like object that appeared to have a miniature galaxy inside it. "What does this do? Looks like some kind of galactic map or something." I tried to peer inside it by putting it right up to my face.

"You know very well what that is, now put it down." She carried on typing on her invisible keyboard and occasionally pinching and twisting the air in from of her screen.

"So, um, have you guys been able to cook up another one of those kronometers which can go undetected by that pesky satellite?" I asked, thinking about the last one I handed to Charlie.

She paused. "Erm, I don't know Zee. Is this information you need for any particular reason? Not to mention, it's none of your business anymore." She suddenly seemed nervous.

"Yea, maybe? I mean I just want to know if you guys are

still making those things. Never really understood why they needed to be made in the first place I guess. Oh hey, does the government know?"

She shifted on her desk occasionally throwing a questioning look in my direction. I could sense her unease.

"Ok, I'm sorry Kate, but listen I do have one important question for you if you can give me just a teeny tiny second of your time." I said, putting down the tesseract. "What is *really* going on here? I mean because I heard the FTL drives were some sort of cover for something far bigger." I said, while pretending to practice my golf swing.

Kate looked at me and let out a large sigh. "Ok Zee, what do you know? You are getting into something way above your head. I would suggest you back down or you are going to end up dead." She paused to take a few calming breaths. "This is—"

I felt presence on my shoulder, a hand.

"Ah, There you are Zee, we thought we'd lost you." It was Colonel Fairservice.

Ah, There you are Colonel, I thought I'd lost you. Perfect timing as usual," the sarcasm was thick in my voice.

"I hope your little excursion here wasn't some half arsed attempt at escaping was it now." He said, smirking. "It's time for you to come with us to see the Director. Try not to get lost this time please."

"Ready when you are Colonel, lead the way." I gave Kate a wink as I turned and headed for the door ahead of Colonel Fairservice.

SEVEN

AD 2775 - July 28 - Zee

"Daayamm!" I exclaimed, giving a low whistling sound as I stepped into the Director's office just behind Colonel Fairservice and Colonel Fone. "What in the name of Marvin is this magnificent place? It's unbelievable!" I said excitedly, taking in my surroundings. It was a large hexagonal room with a giant window on the far side which overlooked the hanger with the floating space orbs that I was just in. The ceiling was clear, revealing a beautiful view of outer space. Tiny tube like pipes, almost invisible, which could easily be mistaken for a form of design, ran around some parts of the glass and down the walls and judging by the taste of the amazingly refreshing air quality, my guess was that these were air filters.

I took a few steps forwards towards the window which overlooked the hangar. Awestruck, I could see the FTL prototypes again, this time from above. It seemed as if it was bending light around it or something similar, because its edges were fading into invisibility. A little bit like when you put a pen into a glass of water and it appears to be in a totally different place that it actually is.

"Hey, Zee, the Director isn't going to be happy if he comes in and finds your dribble all over his nice clean floor. Try and close your mouth there if you can, the cleaners are having a day off today." Fone said to me, clearly impressed by the prototype himself. Though in my defence, one doesn't get to see something this incredible everyday. I also noted that usually, Colonel Fone sounded strangely intelligent there for a moment, impressive.

"Finally, something relatively sardonic from you!" I exclaimed and continued, "Too bad it would probably take another thousand of years or so for you to bring up something alike." I said, giving him a smug look.

Fone's satisfied smile on his face, became a frown, then his nose flared as red as a ripe tomato plant. His expression was priceless.

"Relax, We're even mate." I said, winking at him.

From the look of it, it took Fone enough willpower to keep him from charging at me just to wipe off the smug look off my face.

"One of these days Zee, I promise you, one of these d—"

"Argh-Ehhem," Fairservice, who had been the quiet spectator of the banter all along, cleared his throat to remind us both where we were. And as if on cue, a door shaped hole in the wall to the left of us opened up and through the darkness, out stepped the Director.

"Well, if it isn't the infamous Zee Anderson!" The director said slowly and calmly, as he walked out of the doorway and confidently strode towards us.

Honestly, I guess I had expected an elderly man of some sort. This guy wasn't the stereotypical bond villain type that I fully presumed to be the Director. His clean cut suit did a good job at flaunting his moderate sized muscle and his athletic figure. I needed no seer to know well enough that he had been hitting the gym. I eyed him jealously as I tried recalling the last time I visited a gym…

Though his body gave off the vibe of a man in his twenties, I figured, he probably took his first serum shot in his thirties judging from the not too obvious, but definitely there, mature lines decorating his face.

Out of nowhere I suddenly had a wave of adrenaline

sweeping through my entire body. Was this the man who gave the order to send agents into the mine? Is this man a cold blooded murderer? Is he going to kill me right now? I shuffled my feet and looked around the room taking slow deep breaths to try and steady my nerves. The director gave a curt nod to the agents as he approached, they nodded in response and filed out of the room, leaving just myself and the Director.

"Nice office sir, stunning view." Trying to kill the awkward silence.

"Mmm indeed, though it has to be said that this view would a whole lot better once we are done with this project. We are close Zee, very close." The Director replied, pride deeply laced in his voice.

I dragged my attention back to the unique looking spaceship that was floating majestically above the hangar floor below us, whilst trying to restrain myself from saying something stupid. This was the Director of LINGER I was with now, not Fone or Fairservice, I thought to myself.

"Like what you see, huh?" The Director asked noticing that I was still astounded at what was before me, and without waiting for my response, he continued.

"She is a masterpiece Zee. She'll be able to visit far away stars and even galaxies. Once this baby is finished, the entire universe will be our playground, and perhaps alternate universes and dimensions. Who knows what lies in front of us Zee, worlds that we can only dream of. The very fabric of reality will be changed forever." He looked at me waiting for some kind of response. I had nothing. "I designed her you know. Not to discredit any of the other people involved in this project. We have some of the best engineers, software developers, technicians and physicists in the solar system to get the thing working, but the design, thats mine."

Ok, so he's proud of himself, nothing wrong with that I guess.

"When we began the FTL project, no one ever saw the possibility of it being a reality. It was dismissed as a pipe dream, a fools paradise, a pie in the sky if you will, except me Zee, except me." He continued as he moved towards the sphere shaped aircraft that had LINGER written in black on the side of its silver shimmering body.

"Isn't she a beauty?"

A rhetorical question, I knew there was not really any word better to describe the magnificent structure in front of us. But just to get him piqued, I replied. "I guess so, yes." The director just waved off my reply with a light chuckle, and continued.

"You know, whenever I set my mind to get something done, I do all I can to get it done, no matter what it takes. Because I don't believe in the word failure." The Director said, emphasising on the second to the last phrase which caught my interest.

"No matter what it takes, huh?" I muttered to myself.

"Did you say something?" Director asked, as he turned to face me.

"No, not at all..." I lied, as I began moving around the room, as though admiring the decor and I found myself stopped at a shelf which was filled with various awards, some real, some holographic. "Very Impressive." I said, turning towards him.

"They are trash Zee." He said almost angrily. "Meaningless junk. What matters is what we do in our lives, not what we have sitting on our shelves. I used to think these awards meant something to me, but I now know they are nothing more than just clutter."

I though it best to try and bring the subject back to the FTL ships.

"So, what inspired the FTL project?" I asked, leaning back onto a half wall to get comfortable while waiting for the Director to tell his hopefully short tale.

He came over to where I was standing, stared at me for a few moments before deciding that his tale would sound better if he paced around the room. So off he went.

"As a small child, watching the stars and the heavenly bodies from my bedroom window, it had always being a desire, a dream, a burning ambition not just to travel to the stars, but explore the whole galaxy and the universe."

He stopped at a small model solar system, flicking the planet Venus to send it spinning around and around. I, meanwhile, couldn't get the image of the Director as small boy, looking out his window.

"When the governments began colonising the other planets," he started, turning back towards me. "We all believed it was for a good cause, the best cause. At least, our ability to reach the other planets and colonise them quashed the fear of humans ever going extinct on Earth. It just wouldn't be of any concern anymore, just think of how the human race could advance itself spiritually and socially without the constant burden of self extinction. But we were blinded by their sweet talk to see their real motive." He continued, resentment clearly laced in his voice. "When the project was completed, or so we thought. We naively didn't think the governments would be greedy enough to plot a scheme with some of the major corporations at the time, to control the necessary materials needed for such travel just for themselves, while also only using the cheapest materials possible and putting thousands, if not millions of lives in danger. As the first set of humans were sent out to the planets, as *'lab rats'* to taste colonisation of other worlds. The world applauded and praised our governmental overlords. However, after a few short years of habitation, one by one there were breaches of all the reactors keeping the people safe on these planets."

"And the people, what happened to the people?" I asked, genuinely curious, with a little hope too, maybe.

"Most died, suffocation, cancers or starvation. Those who survived, had their immune system destroyed or their DNA mutated so badly that their bodies couldn't function for long, there were a lot of horrible slow and painful deaths." After a slight pause, Director continued in a slightly lowered voice. "I lost someone on Venus due the greed and ineptness of the governments who swore to protect." I saw a brief glint of sadness in his eyes and something which seemed like regret, but this was immediately hidden, as though it was never there.

That explains his unfathomable hatred for the governments, I thought.

He turned to face me "So, I understand how you feel Zee." Director finished, as he turned back to face me, came closer and patted me on my shoulder.

Wait what? I thought…

"What do you mean by that sir?" I eyed him suspiciously.

"Well, I've never had the luxury to feel the love of a father, but I know exactly how it feels when you lose a loved one to the cold hands of death, especially if there is a known force behind it." He said, staring back out of the window once more. "Charlie will be exposed to grave danger if you do not release him from this path you have set him on. Oh, I know Winston told you things. They aren't true. Winston was a traitor. Now, you haven't exactly been very loyal to LINGER either," his eyes were intensely fixed on mine "So, I have a mission for you that you really don't have much choice but to accept."

"Ok," I was becoming quite frightened by this point. "Go

on."

"You must take Charlie back to his original timeline, eliminating him from the equation. This will then leave us open to then find out what Winston's real motives were. Once you have done this, I would like to you return back here to the moon-base and continue your operations alongside us, heavily supervised of course. But if you fail, you will spend an eternity behind bars in permeant solitude and in complete darkness. I do hope I am making myself clear Zee." The Director took a slight pause, and continued in a much more soothing voice. "LINGER does of course take some responsibility for the death of your father, but Zee, as you very well know by now, the past can't be changed under any circumstances, no matter how hard you want to try."

LINGERLUST

EIGHT

BC 399 - August 16 - Charlie

We were exhausted to the bones when we arrived the outskirts of Sparta. "It would probably be better we wait here for a while." Hekate said. "We wouldn't want to attract any unnecessary attention to ourselves just yet."

While on our way here, Hekate had explained that the Spartans and Athenians weren't quite on the best terms at the moment. The two were warring some years back and quite a few Athenians were captured, and are still held captive right here in Sparta. There were also other Greeks captured from other territories conquered by Sparta, and here they were referred to as Helots, slaves basically. This is something we would rather avoid becoming.

We arrived at a small inn, strangely the inn-keeper had been expecting us. I wondered if this might have been Plato's doing? Though how he managed to send word out here before we got here ourselves, I don't know.

Regardless, we attached the reigns of the horses to some wooden poles outside the inn and removed our bags. The inn-keeper gestured us in through the main door which lead into an outdoor central atrium area.

"This one, your room." He pointed towards a small curved wooden door closest to us. At least he was direct I thought, good, I was shattered.

Once inside the room, I dropped my bag and dragged myself directly to the bed. It felt surprisingly soft and very comfortable once my back landed on it, causing my body to relax instantly. Forgetting that I was still fully clothed, I drifted off to sleep.

***

I woke to the morning suns rays shining through the window directly into my eyes. "Oh my god, that is bright!" Trying to use the back of my palm to fend off the fiendish things as I used the other hand to help prop me up.

"Well well, the princess awakes." Came a familiar voice, which obviously belonged to Hekate. I turned myself sideways on the bed so I could touch the ground with my feet and stretched my limbs, which where still aching like hell. "What time is it?" I asked, sitting upright, rubbing my eyes with my whole hands.

"Time enough to get you off that bed, perhaps to begin the task at hand." Came another voice from the opposite side of the room.

"Plato?" I asked sitting bolt upright, searching the room until my eyes finally landed on him bent over in front of a leather sack, clearly trying to retrieve something or other from it.

"When the hell did you arrive?" I asked.

"Well, If you hadn't been sleeping like a corpse, you might well have noticed him coming in earlier this morning." Hekate spoke for Plato, standing in front of me with his arms folded across his chest.

"Well Charlie, I calculated that you might need an extra hand, so I took off in your direction not so long after you two left actually." Plato said, offering a brief smile. "But I very much doubt I spent as much time as you two dilly dallying along the way."

"Oh yes, an extra hand, thank you very mu—". I started but was cut off half way by Plato. "No need to, in all honesty, I'm actually just honouring my teacher's last wish." He was deadpan. The tension was suddenly thick, I doubt a chainsaw would have made it through.

"Um, hey listen—is there anywhere I can go to wash up around here?" I awkwardly asked, trying and failing to break the silent tension.

"Upfront and on your left, you'll see a single stall." Hekate nodded towards the a passageway. "...And breakfast will probably be here shortly, so if you want any, you'd better make it quick."

I followed the directions Hekate had just given me and made my way through the small passageway. I could see on my left a small indentation in the wall followed by a pungent smell. This must be the place then. I noticed a tiny well-like structure, just beside the stall and a small clay pot which I assumed was use to scoop the water from the well. It didn't take a genius to know that the water and water pot was for. I scooped up water from the well and stepped into the indentation, shutting a small wooden door behind me. The thought of how the people of old, stood in a this manner just to release some toxic waste made me cringe. This hole didn't look safe enough and the thought of a reptile crawling out from it made me hasten my business. I washed up quickly and wiped up with the linen that was conveniently left on the side and got myself out of this place as fast as I could, leaving the water pot in the stall.

When I got back to the room, breakfast was set on the table already, with Plato and Hekate sitting looking at me, clearly awaiting my arrival before digging in.

"That was quick." Hekate said, rolling his eyes.

I stared at the food in front of us on the table, unsure of what I was actually looking at. "This looks nice." I said, sporting one of those unavoidable fake smiles.

"These creations are called tiganites." Hekate spoke with supreme confidence. "They are like a sort of what *you* might call a pancake. These ones though are made with wheat flour, olive oil, honey, and curdled milk. You'll love them, dig in."

Unlike the hard bread we ate back in Athens, the tiganites were surprisingly soft and there was no need to dip in the goblet of wine that each of us had on the table. Clearly alcoholic beverages for breakfast were a thing here in ancient Greece.

For the next five minutes or so, we ate in silence and pretty much ignored each other entirely. The only sound that could be heard was that of munching, the occasional grunt or burp and the clanking of goblets banging back down onto the table. Once he was done, Hekate rang a tiny bell in the middle of the table, which I initially hadn't noticed before. In the blink of an eye a gentleman in the cleanest, brightest, whitest robes you're ever likely to see, entered the room, cleared up the table in seconds and disappeared back through the archway in the wall, thus bringing the room back to the state it was before I left for the bathroom.

I decided I needed to speak, mustering up some courage, I stood up from the table, backing away slightly and began. "Plato, Hekate, listen, there is something I feel I need to say to you before we carry on with our mission. I think its important that there are no bad feelings between us, as we've got to be able to work together flawlessly in the coming few days. I'm so very sorry for the loss of your teacher and mentor, Socrates." I pleaded, with my hands folded together in front of my face. "He was a man set in his ways, but I did all that was possible to try and help during that awful time."

Plato stood and rested his hand on my shoulder. "Charlie, It's ok, it's ok." "We are fully aware the death of Socrates wasn't in any way a fault of yours. The gods decided his fate and there is nothing we can do for him now but fulfil his wishes and accept his death as part of his conscious story in this universe, so we can all move on with ours."

Plato said, reassuringly. The feeling of relief that swept over me was very welcome.

"Thank you Plato, that means a lot more to me that I can put into words. I wouldn't want to be held accountable for the death of one of the greatest men to ever life." I said, suddenly thinking that I might have sounded a little selfish.

Plato gave a small grunt and returned to his seat at the table. "Socrates mentioned that you seek a substance located at the quarry of Viglafia, not far from here. This, for now, is all I know. Can you tell us anything further that might aid is in obtaining this?" Plato gave the impression he thought I already knew the location of the terbimanium.

"Right. Viglafia. Quarry. Ok yes, thank you I will. I can't go into too many details unfortunately. You'll just need to trust me that getting to the deposit in good time is important, really really important. Not just for us, but for the future of the world and the lives that will be saved if we do indeed manage to destroy this substance. I would love to go into details, but I honestly don't know them. The only thing I can tell you is that the substance is called terbimanium. It's a metal, but its natural form is a liquid. I know that it sounds like I am asking you to take a huge leap of faith and just blindly trust the words I am saying. But If that liquid metal gets into the wrong hands, believe me there are a lot of wrong hands in this world, millions of people will be in mortal danger." It felt for a moment like I was pitching for a client contract at work.

"You know we are in this together Charlie. So, what is our next move?" Plato replied after a brief moment of silence while Hekate just gave an affirmative nod.

"So, as far as I am aware, and please correct me if I am way off here. The Spartans were, I mean *are* made of three classes of people, The Spartiates are basically the citizens of Sparta, the Perioeci, who are in essence foreigners but with pretty much the same rights as the perioeci right?" Hekate, gave me a thumbs up. "There is also the Helots. As I am told, these guys are the slaves of Sparta and are the people most likely to be working in the quarry. So, to get to the main deposit source, we need to blend in like the Helots. We would get in perhaps during the slaves lunch or somethi—"

"Lunch break? The slaves are not privileged to that kind of luxury." Hekate interrupted.

"Okay, their break or whatever. You know, a short period they are allowed to rest. Surely they get one of those?" I said.

"Ah yes," Hekate said excitedly, "there are official rules which do state that during the Helots' break-time, they are asked to leave the quarry to drink some water at the brook, stretch their legs or have a lie down to rest. But not one of them is expected to be inside the quarry during this time."

I paused a moment to reflect on this for a short moment, then an idea popped into my head. "Right! OK. So when all the Helots file out, one of us will go distract the guard in charge. Then while the guards attention is diverted, the remaining two will attempt to sneak into the quarry unnoticed." There was a pause again, while everyone pondered.

"Their break is probably only for about ten minutes, do you think this would be enough time to get in and destroy the terbinami—"

"Terbimanium."

"Yes, that, do you think ten minutes is enough time to fully distract an on duty guard and get into the quarry?" Hekate asked.

"It has to be enough time." I said, having no idea whether it was enough or not. "Otherwise we'd probably all end up locked up in a four walled stone cube for a very, very long time."

Hekate got up and walked over to the corner where his linen was, pulled out a small brown pot, some flat wooden like object, some rolled up hard reed and placed them all on the table.

"What is this called?" I pointed at the paper like material, "Papyrus." Hekate said, dipping the wooden object into the small brown pot, which contained some form of ink.

Hekate began. "The last time I came here was during one of the compass demonstrations that the Spartans were showing off. The demonstration was held inside the quarry just outside a small cave entrance, so from my guess, the ternibami—thingy deposit isn't far from there, in fact I would go so far as to say, the thingy is in that cave." Hekate said, as he began to draw the outline of the quarry, then a cave like entrance on one side. "There is also a lake just beside the entrance to the quarry." He drew an outline of the lake. "This is where the Helots will go on their break, and here—" He then prodded the reed onto the paper right at the entrance to the quarry, " is where our guard will be." His drawings were actually outstanding, quite the artistic perfectionist is Hekate it seems.

"Now, when we arrive at the quarry, we will wait at this part of the lake," he tapped on a particular spot beside the lake on our newly created map. "Once the Helots leave the quarry for their break, they will, more than likely, head to the lake so we will need to quickly blend in, then move over towards the entrance. Plato, you will distract the guard somehow while Charlie and I will sneak past and head into the quarry towards the cave, any questions?" He asked, and carefully placed the reed back on the table.

"Yeah, I have one." I said, raising my hand like a shy school-kid. "What if the terbimanium actually isn't in this cave?"

"Then I guess we will become permanent residents of this quarry as helots." Hekate said, unable to prevent a smirk before continuing. "Okay then, since there is no real questions, and everyone seems to understand the plan almost perfectly, let's pack our bags up and head out." Hekate stood up and stretched his arms right around his back.

"Right, it's a plan then." I replied, banging the table with my fist, knocking the down ink pot all over Platos' nice clean white robes.

* * *

***

The midnight rain beat down on us relentlessly, and three bumpy, wet and thoroughly miserable hours later, we arrived at the edge of the lake, on the opposite side to the entrance to the quarry. We had decided to dress as some perioeci, the idea being that we wouldn't attract any unnecessary attention on the way. Plato figured that no one would give much heed to non-citizens of Sparta just passing though.

We stayed at a safe distance from the quarry entrance to change into our helot outfits. How Hekate had managed to acquire these is something I would rather not think about. We tied our horses to a nearby tree in the woods, just out of sight and I removed my backpack and slotted it underneath my smelly helot clothes. I suddenly caught the fear of potentially losing my bag, what if someone else from Ancient Greece got their hands on it? The chain of events that could occur just don't bare thinking about.

Hekate signalled to the both of us that the coast was clear to move in closer. We moved in close enough so we could get a clearer view of the entrance but stay out of sight. The three of us shuffled through the grass to a nearby boulder and hid behind it. Hekate slowly poked his head over the rock to get a better look.

"Helots! Our timing is perfect. They are coming out of the quarry towards the lake. Now is our chance." He bellowed in his loudest whisper. "Ready Plato?"

Plato glanced at Hekate and then over towards the entrance. "Ok, I'm ready, wait for my signal."

Plato moved from our hiding spot and calmly walked passed the incoming helots and over towards entrance. As we watched him walk towards the guard, my nerves began to run riot. Maybe I should have spent a little longer in that toilet cupboard.

"Hey! You! Turn yourself around!" Came a stern voice from the guard.

Plato still moved on towards the guard. It seemed as if he was trying to explain some kind of a situation to the guard, but from the looks of it, the guard wasn't having any of it and was still insisting Plato turn back. Once Plato got close enough, he stopped in front of the guard who was still shouting and pointing with a sharp looking spear towards to lake, and with a perfectly timed move, he snatched the spear from the hand of the guard and took off running, forcing the guard to run after him. Woah! Okay, I didn't expect that, but I'm guessing that is his signal for us to move.

"Go! Now" Hekate shouted in his quietest whisper voice.

We picked ourselves up and ran towards the entrance of the quarry, the guard and Plato disappearing in the opposite direction. Easy enough, we were able to gain entry without any resistance at all.

Inside, it was dark, really dark. We couldn't see more than just a few feet in front of us. I wondered how the hell these guys could see what they were doing in here? I pulled off my bag and rummaged around inside searching for a flashlight or a lighter something helpful. As luck would have it, I found two tiny pen torches. I switched them on and handed one to Hekate.

Hekate took the torch from me. "Are you not expecting me to ask what on earth this is you've just handed me Charlie?" He paused. "You would do well not to reveal this kind of technology to the folk around here." His eyes pierced deep into my soul. I could feel the panic fast setting in.

"I know where you are from, Charlie, and it would be best if it is not spoken of again, at least for now anyway."

"Who are you?" My voice quivering with anxiety.

"That's for later Charlie, we have a job to do here don't we?"

I could feel my heart beating like a bongo drum. Does this guy work for L.I.N.G.E.R? Is he a friend of Zee? Can I trust him? Is he going to kill me? I had thousands of questions whizzing around my head, but I decided to try and push them to the back of mind until we were out of here.

"There! Look." Hekate pointed towards a narrow opening in between a few of the rocks that were scattered around the at the base of the quarry. "That's the cave."

We carefully made our way down the shallow slope towards the cave. As we approached the entrance, we quickly realised that we had to get on hands and knees to get into it. But once we were in, it opened up into a large open cave. After maybe only a few minutes of making our way though cave puddles and squeezing though tiny claustrophobic gaps in rocks Hekate halted, I walked into the back of him.

"Shhh, I hear something." He said, concentrating, as if trying to catch a faint sound of something.

"What's that?" I whispered, hoping it wasn't a snake or any some other kind of ancient cave monster which was definitely going to eat us both.

"Voices," he whispered back. I quieted down to try and hear the same, then I heard it, like faint sounds of a conversation further up ahead.

"This way," Hekate said, slowly following the faint sound until we came to a steep rock face rising up as far as we could see in front of us. "Dam! Dead end."

"Shit!" I said, when I immediately became aware of something dripping on me. I tilted my head towards the wet patch on my shoulder and used my finger to see what it was. The substance was sticky to start with but it rapidly began to solidify until it became a tiny silver pebble in my hand.

"Oh my G— I think I've found it!" I whispered excitedly to Hekate. I pointed my pen torch upwards to see where the substance was coming from. I could see the shapes of some large wooden barrels, clearly where the terbimanium was leaking out of. I also noticed small flat planks, suspended from ropes on the both sides of the wood which were connected somehow to the top of the barrels. I figured that they would lower and raise the barrels, maybe to retrieve the liquid which was flowing into them from inside the cave walls.

"See that up there." I gestured towards the barrels. "That's gotta be it."

"Yeah, I see it." He said, turning to me. "So now what?" Turning his head back up towards the suspended barrels.

"I guess we have to blow them up somehow, I'm not sure, but I think this stuff is fairly flammable. There's got to be something in my bag we can use to destroy it." I said, spinning my backpack around and setting it on the cave floor.

"Who goes there?" Came a shout that seemed to come from behind us as we heard footsteps starting to approach our location.

"No! We've been heard. Grab your bag Charlie, we have to get out of sight now!" Hekate had a sense of urgency in his voice if not heard before. I grabbed my bag up and slung it on my back once again.

"Shit shit shit" was all I could think so say.

"Quick, this way," he whispered frantically, taking his torch, snatching mine and smashing them both on the ground. He then turned and led the way back through the cave tunnel.

"Hide!" Hekate shoved me into a tiny crevice in the side of the tunnel wall. I found myself standing with my back to the rocks with Hekate pushing himself hard up against me. "Shh, they are right here. Stay quiet."

I almost forgot to breathe as I heard the guards walking and talking inches away from where we were hiding. Slowly Hekate carefully bent down and picked up a small stone which he threw down into the tunnel ahead of the guards. The stone made a light clunking clicking sound as it pinged around the inside of the cave tunnel.

"What was that? Who is there?" One of the guards shouted again, as they quickened their pace towards the direction of the noise. Hekate grabbed me by the collar and dragged me off the wall, then began running blindly back to the entrance in the pitch darkness hoping that we didn't make a wrong turn and wind up in the arms of an ancient cave yeti. Thankfully, we managed to reach the entrance to the cave and noticed the helots slowing filing back into the quarry.

"Now is our chance, head towards the helots as fast as you can, go straight passed them and get out of this quarry. Go!" The tone of Hekates' voice was desperate.

Somehow, we did manage to get out of the quarry entrance unseen by any of the guards. Plenty of the Helots saw us bolting passed them though, I half expected them to start following us, thinking we were starting some kind of revolution. We headed straight back towards the side of the lake where we had tied our horses and changed our clothes. Plato was already there, sitting on the ground beside his horse reading some kind of manuscript. He had already changed back into to his Perioeci clothes.

"Took you guys long enough." He said as he closed his paper and hauled himself to his feet. "Did you find what you were looking for?"

"We found it." I said, trying to catch my breath. "But we had to get out of there before we could destroy it."

"Why? What happened?" Plato asked as he shot up to a standing position.

"The terbimanium is almost certainly located inside a small cave to the side of the quarry. We managed to get inside and locate the exact position of it. But before we could do anything about it, we were busted by a couple of guards." I said, my breath was now fully caught. Thank goodness for Hekates' quick thinking, or I'm sure we would have been a permanent resident of that quarry for sure.

"Well, I am very glad you are both alive." Plato started, "however, try not to be too disheartened just yet, as there is always Hyakinthia".

I was walking towards my horse and stopped dead in my tracks.

"Hyakinthia?" I asked, my eyes wide with curious excitement.

"Yes, that is what I said. I hear a tale of another one of those compass demonstrations during the Hyakinthia festival in two days time. Now, while the main part of this festival is actually held in Sparta, I would propose that the compass demonstration will actually be held right here, in that quarry. "He pointed towards the entrance. "I propose we set up camp a little further into those woods and wait until the Spartan public are invited back to the quarry area to view the demonstration. That way, we can get in without having to sneak about."

NINE

BC 399 - August 19 - Charlie

We kept a close eye on the group of strange men we noticed at the demonstration, they sat across from us at the bonfire which was part of the Hyakinthia festival. There was dancing, fire juggling and all sorts of bizarre performances in and around the quarry area. So far, we were doing a pretty good job of blending in to our surroundings.

Hekate was the first to notice the men going in and out of the cave where we were sure the deposit was located.

"Guys." He said, nudging us both with his elbows and pointing in the direction of four men, who were stood around, seemingly just talking to each other. "I don't think those men are Spartans or even Perioecis."

Plato and I turned towards them to get a better look.

"What makes you say that?" I said, having no real idea of

the difference between most of these people anyway.

"Well, look at them, they are certainly not helots, they are wearing stitched wool, no helot can afford that type of dress. If they are Spartiates, then they wouldn't have warrior brooches on their straps." Hekate rubbed his chin, clearly in detective mode. "I don't know, something's not right here." He said, shaking his head.

The men wore a heavy rectangular woollen dress, Hekate had called a tunic or an exomis, fastened with a large wooden brooch on their left shoulder strap. They also and they wore roman style gladiator sandals on their feet.

"Those tunics are supposed to be fastened on the right hand side, and the length for men is supposed to be knee length, these are far too short. There should also be a belt or rope tied around their waists and their tunics should reach their ankles. The way these men are dressed is centuries old." Hekate paused as his eyes followed their movements. "An exomis, that's very odd, besides the fact they have it strapped to their left arms, its only worn when a spartan is on horseback, for racing and such, doing some exercise or some form of hard labour." Hekate concluded, his eyes fixated on them.

My mind began to race, what if these guys are LINGER

agents? Here solely to recover the terbimanium deposits and return them to their future and kill anyone in their way. We then noticed that they were moving away from us and headed directly towards the cave entrance.

"I say we follow them." I suggested to Hekate.

"Yes, I agree with that suggestion. Something is not quite adding up here." Plato said, standing and slowly turning the to face the opposite direction of the men in a strange and overly obvious and terrible attempt to be discreet.

As the men reached a safe enough distance, the three of us began to follow. Sure enough they were headed for the cave. But just stopped just at the entrance and made a slight deviation to the right of it and stopped.

"Wait here." Hekate said quietly, "they are stopping. Maybe they are waiting for something." We found ourselves a little dark spot somewhere in between the bonfire and the cave entrance and sat down on the ground to see what their next move might be.

"Hey, Charlie, seems you've got yourself an admirer." Hekate nudged me with his shoulder and used his head to point in the direction of the bonfire. I tried to figure out who the hell he was referring to when my eyes came in contact with hers.

She was absolutely stunning, not like the women you see in some of those ridiculous magazines. This woman had a natural beauty, large pretty eyes, and her head was shaved completely bald.

"Hekate, She's got no hair! I mean, why is her hair cut so short?" I asked, trying to point discreetly towards the top of her head.

Hekate burst into a child like snigger. "For you Charlie, she is a no no, and I mean—no." Hekate gave Plato a gently elbow nudge to try and get him involved. "She is pretty much a married woman my friend."

"Pretty much? How on earth do you know that?" I asked, obviously out of pure curiosity. "I don't see any rings on her fingers or anything like that."

"So, once a spartan woman is about to get married, her hair is shaved completely off her scalp, it's part of the marriage preparation I suppose."

Plato, who had been quiet for most of the conversation chimed in. "Judging by the situation happening around her middle area, I would presume that this lady is already married."

"Oh yes," I saw immediately what Plato was referring to.

"Hey, have you guys noticed that pretty much all the women here look like they could out run a cheetah. I mean, they all look a lot more athletic than say, y'know—" I used my hand to draw an invisible curvy shape on the air. "Any reason why that might be?" I asked, looking at them both, while they both looked back at me like I was some kind of weirdo.

"Well, if you keep drinking this stuff here," Plato began, picking up the cup I had been sipping from. "You'll end up more drunk than you already seem. Perhaps you have had enough of this, being drunk is something that spartans are not very impressed with." Plato placed back the cup to its former position on the ground while Hekate gave a little chuckle.

"Why? What am I drinking? I thought it was just some kind of berry juice or something like that right?"

"It's wine! By the grace of Apollo, have you never tasted wine before?" Plato suddenly seemed a little agitated. "Anyway, to answer your earlier question. Spartan males are expected to start up training to become soldiers and warriors from the age of seven years old, the Agoge, very rigorous. So as well as the males, the females are also trained. They are shown how to throw the javelin and learn to wrestle proficiently. The idea is to get them ready for having children I believe, which I have always found utterly preposterous, but it's true. Aside from this, the women of Sparta are excellent singers and dancers too." Plato explained.

I found myself sitting very attentively, as if I was being told a bedtime story.

"You can drop down that hand of yours too, we aren't in a classroom." Plato pointed to my raised hand which I immediately dropped, not realising that I even had it raised in the first place.

"But I have another question. Where is the Agoge?" Plato breathed a sigh of frustration before replying.

"Agoge, is not a place, it is a training program, like a course if you will, where Spartan male folks from the age of seven, are taken to begin learning their extremely disciplined and rigorous state sponsored education, military training and social skills. It is said to be the toughest training known to both man and gods. By the age of twenty, they will become full Spartan warriors and will often be sent to participate in slaying some poor Greeks. If they make it to the age of thirty, they are briefly allowed to leave the barracks to get married, but they will still be in service until the age of sixty. Does this answer your question?" Plato finished, dismissively.

"I think we need to go now." Hekate said as he stood up in a rush. "Those men are leaving the area, we need to see where they are going." Plato staggered slightly as he rose. I tried to give him a helping hand, but he completely dismissed it.

"Don't worry, I'm fine. Let's go."

The moon shone brightly, lighting our way as we discreetly followed closely behind the strangers. They were further away from the cave following the sides of the rock cliff to the right. Hekate lead us around a small pit and through a small lake full of sludge. We continued following the men until we came to a slight hill.

"We can see what they are up to from here." Hekate said, laying down on his font.

The men came to a small round tent about fifty feet away from the entrance to the cace. Two of them went inside while the other two seemed to wait outside, standing guard.

"Do you think they have the terbimanium in that tent." I asked, waiting for anyone to answer.

"Quiet Charlie." Came my only response, from Hekate of course.

When they finally exited the tent about ten minutes later, the two men were carrying a large wooden barrel, using two large wooden planks on either side to keep it level.

"That's the barrel!" I shouted, losing complete control over the volume of my voice.

"Sshht—quiet!" This time Hekate's hands were firmly planted over my mouth.

These guys must be from from LINGER and I'm sure it wouldn't be long before they would somehow have the barrel out of here and far into the future. I entered into panic mode.

"Damnit! Shit shit shit! I've screwed it up again!" I said, shoving Hekate's hand away from my face in frustration and wildly running my fingers through my hair.

"Hey hey, come-on now, it's not even close to being over just yet." I looked up at Plato, who had his arm stretched out as if he help me off the ground. "Okay," Plato began. "That barrel definitely looks flammable, and I would bet my life's belongings that the contents are too. One of us needs to head down the hill and retrieve one of those burning torches over there." He motioned towards the bonfire, which was surrounded by burning torches planted into the ground. "While the others head down to distract those men away from that container somehow."

"And what are we supposed to do once the barrel is up in flames?" I said

"Run." Plato said. "It worked for me before, it will work again."

"Run? Right, run. Are you sure that thing is flammable?"

"No."

"Great! This is the perfect plan. So who is doing what then?" I asked as Plato and I both stared at Hekate's direction. "Charlie, this is your mission, you head down ahead of us and get hold of one of those burning torches, but keep it discreet ok. Once we are sure you have one and are in a good position, We will make our way towards the men to distract them." Hekate said, as he put both his hands on each of my shoulders. For some reason, this felt like a goodbye.

Plato motioned towards one of the burning torches on the far side of the bonfire. "Head towards that one over there, it seems like the best place for you to be."

"Right then" I paused to take a deep breath. "Here goes."

I crouched down and slowly made my way back down towards the fire and the torch on the far side, being extra careful not to accidentally kick any loose rocks or stones on the way down, when I could have sworn I head Platos' voice saying something incoherent. I turned around towards Plato and Hekate at the top of the hill to try and confirm my suspicions, when I felt bang on the back of my head.

I could feel myself falling to the ground in slow motion, my body separated from my mind. Everything suddenly felt like a vivid dream. I dreamt of a pair of hands catching me before I could I hit the ground, then

darkness.

TEN

AD 1912 - April 9 - Charlie

Slowly, I managed to open my heavy eyes. A painted white ceiling presented itself, with a light bulb blinking like it was trying to give me some kind of important morse code message about what the hell was going on in my life right now.

"Ow, my head," I hissed at the searing pain shooting through my neck and up to the top of my head. It felt like either my brain had exploded, or was about to. With a great deal of effort, I lifted myself up to see where the hell I was. The room was small, dingy and had a definite smell of fish. The whole room was basically a four walled bookcase, books were everywhere. Immediately to my right was a small coffee table with a candle and a glass of what looked like water, though had a slight tint of brown. I raised my hand up to see if I could feel anything that might be causing the pain in my head. Bandages.

"Wait what?!" I jumped off the bed and fell straight to the floor with a loud thud. How did I get here? Why is there a bandage around my head? Was there blood? I hate blood, please don't let there be any blood.

"Now now young man, getting yourself up so soon like that will just worsen the pain my dear." Came an elderly and feminine voice. I jerked my head towards the direction from which the voice had come from, regretting it almost immediately as it doubled the pain. A woman, probably in her late sixties, or early seventies and wearing a mid-shin length dress was standing, slightly bent over in the corner of the room. In fact it seemed that this was the only part of the room which wasn't a library. The woman was standing over a small kettle which was whistling with steam. Slowly, I managed to picked myself up off the floor and carefully place myself back onto the bed.

"Where am I? Who are you?" I asked, as I tried getting off the bed again, failed miserably, and fell back on the bed again.

"Relax petal." She said calmly as she came towards me with a mug of boiling something. "Drink this my dear, it will hopefully make you feel a little better," she said, handing the mug over to me. I eyed her suspiciously before taking the mug from her hands.

"Ah, ee, it's hot!"

"Yes, do be careful. Often, tea is quite hot." She had a point.

I looked at the dark looking brown liquid, the dark looking brown liquid looked back at me. I crinkled my nose, as I brought it closer to my lips, expecting it's aroma to cause me to gag. It was wonderful, the best tasting tea I have ever tasted. Just for a fleeting moment, I felt relatively normal.

"My name is Edith." The lady said, as I handed the mug back to her and nodded in acknowledgement. "You've got a nasty bump on your head there. A few more brews and you'll be right as rain I'm sure."

"Thank you, that's really lovely tea." I said, still trying to sit up straight. Man this bed is unbelievably uncomfortable.

I finally managed to get a good look around, I wasn't just in a room but I think that I was actually in the whole house. This was obviously some kind of studio flat. There was a worn out old couch in the middle of the room with some clothes draped all over it. The mini kitchen on the other side and a small door just behind that, which I guess led to a bathroom. The four poster bed I laid on was at the other end of the room.

A cool breeze began blowing in from the small open window that was just above my head. The air had a salty smell to it, like we were close to the sea. It was at this point I remembered the quarry, Plato and Hekate, the cave, the four guys taking the terbimanium and the deafening bang I heard right before I ended up here. I certainly wasn't in Ancient Greece anymore. But I also wasn't back at home safe in the knowledge that all this was just one big crazy dream.

"Edith, do you know where I am?" I asked with a hint of panic in my voice.

"What a strange question to ask." She said, looking at me as though I had lost my mind. "Of course I know where you are, my goodness that bump must have really knock some daylights out of you hey."

"Seriously, where I am?" I asked again, as I slowly turned my body so that my feet could touch the floor.

"You are in my home my dear, in Southampton. I've lived here for over sixty-five years you know, my great gre—."

"Edith, who brought me here."

"Uh, oh yes, why was your—"

"I did!" Came a shout from behind the bathroom door which sounded exactly like mine. Edith shrugged and carried on making more tea in the corner of the room.

"Zee! Is that you in there?" I shouted back, wincing in some more head pain. I heard the toilet flush, then the door slowly creaked open revealing Zee, wiping something off his hands onto his trouser leg.

"Phew, what a relief!" Zee said, walking towards the bed. "I tell you, the amount of sugar I have just consumed has done a serious injustice to my stomach." Rubbing his stomach in relief.

"Zee, I can't tell you how good it feels to see you again." For a moment he felt like my guardian, my rock, someone I could rely on. Someone who got me into this mess in the first bloody place!

"Yeah? So, what's up Charlie? Hows that head of yours hey?" He asked, stretching his hand towards me for a handshake. I eyed his hand and then looked up at his face and back down at his hand again.

"Oh, Sorry, it is clean, promise." He pulled his hand back

and placed it behind his back.

"What the hell happened?" I asked, seeking some kind of information that might make this situation slightly less confusing. "The last thing I remember was walking towards a flaming torch in a quarry in ancient Sparta. I was with Plato and Hekate, we were trying to destroy the terbimanium."

"Yes, Plato and Hekate, I know. I will tell you what happened." Zee said, stroking his chin, thinking, then he gave a long sigh. "What happened Charlie, is you nearly blew your cover!" Zee said angrily.

"You know the most painful part of it?" He looked at me with every ounce of seriousness.

"I did? What did I do wrong?" I asked, almost inaudibly, looking down at the floor.

"The last thing you did Charlie—" He started, I guess he was referring to the moment I went to go and distract the men at the quarry. After a short moment of silence, making me anticipate the next thing he was about to say, he continued.

"Was dam stupid." He was deadpan for a moment. "If those men had seen what you were trying to do, you could have got Hekate and Plato killed. You were never going to be able to destroy that barrel without causing a huge problem for everyone."

"Yea, ok, but I'm pretty sure you would have done the same thing Zee. It's not like we had much choice considering the circumstances we were in." I said, totally forgetting about my banging headache, which amazingly, seemed to have completely disappeared.

"It doesn't matter what I would have done, that's not relevant now. I needed to get you out of there pronto." He said, arranging the collar of his white shirt and an invisible bow-tie.

"Woah woah woah, wait just a second." I said, trying to wrap my mind around something that was very quickly beginning to anger me. "Was it you who bashed me on the back of the head?" I glared at him in the exact way he was glaring at me, literally.

"Errr—yea, it was." He scratched the back of his neck. "Charlie, I was left with no choice. Plus that was the quickest way to get you out of there without any much unnecessary drama. Not to mention the fact that I caught your fall perfectly. You're welcome."

"Shut-up. So now what do we do about the terbimanium?"

I asked, genuinely concerned.

"Well, a teeny tiny sequence of events involving yourself of course, forced me to change plans and gave me no choice but to help LINGER get the terbimanium out from that quarry."

"Yeah right, good one Zee, so you knocked me out cold, then what? Put me in a bush while you gave those men a hand in destroying the universe? This is one of your ridiculous jokes right?" I stared at him in complete disbelief.

"Nope, there wasn't any bushes around. I just left you on the ground. But you should know the terbimanium isn't the only thing LINGER needs to complete their FTL project. They still need some more materials, much rarer ones in fact. The location of which is known to me. So, actually, we are ahead of the game with them at the moment on this one." Zee said nonchalantly. "Also," he raised a broad smile. "Since I've done a good deed in their eyes, hopefully the word will spread around the base and they will be slightly less inclined to come and try and kill us anytime soon, hopefully."

"Yeah, ok I guess that is a fair point. Though I doubt very much that will happen." I said confidently.

Zee bent over and pulled an old brown suitcase from under the bed, slammed it onto the bed with a thud and clicked the latches open one by one.

"Right then, new clothes, check. Kronometers, check, excellent."

He picked up three kronometers and raised them up to his eye level, examining them in the light.

"Yup, these should do. Fully charged." He placed one on his wrist and gave the other one to me. "Put it on and get rid of that old one. The time will set to our location automatically."

After I'd placed the device firmly onto my wrist, Zee sat down on the bed and turned towards me taking a deep breath. "Well, before dragging you on yet another mission, I think I owe you a bit more of an explanation as to whats going on." He then placed the case back on the floor.

"Mmm, yea, that would be nice." I agreed.

"So, as you already know, LINGER needs some raw materials from various parts of the world and in various timelines to complete the work on a particular project they call Faster Than Light—FTL. Actually they call it the SMFTTSOL, but you know, whatever." He shrugged.

"Wait, what's SMFTSL— supposed me mean?" I questioned with a laugh.

"SMFTTSOL — So Much Faster Than the Speed Of Light."

"For real?" I laughed.

"For real, this is L.I.N.G.E.R, of course it's real. Anyway, some many years before the formation L.I.N.G.E.R, a company called SpaceX, who pretty much deal with anything concerning space, convinced governments all over the world, that colonising other planets was a really good idea. Their primary reason being that sending humans off to different places in the solar system to form permanent colonies would prevent the human race from going extinct should anything really bad happen on earth, which of course it did in 2185. So the contract to expand the human race was given to SpaceX, who in turn hired a man, a man who happened to be one of the brightest minds of his generation, in any generation come to think of it. This man aided SpaceX with the terraforming technologies for the colonisation of Mars and Venus in particular. Anyway, To cut a very long story a bit shorter, the man was deceived, all his all work stolen and no credit given to him at all, he was forgotten."

"Jumping forwards by quite a long way now. By the year

2632, the colonisation project was pretty much complete. Humans had entirely terraformed and colonised planet Mars. Mars was now likened to a second Earth and Venus was very close behind."

"In the year 2689, the government had declared Venus completely safe for human habitation. They then asked for volunteers, you know, to see who wants to be the first inhabitants of a new planet and you know how humans are, always eager to try something new, and take over somewhere else. Millions volunteered for the project and pretty much all of them were very soon moved to Venus. Everything they needed on Venus was provided. It was like a paradise, perfect in every way. Perfect until the reactor which was keeping the atmospheric pressure stable and the air breathable, failed. The failure of the reactor was deemed to be as a result of governmental negligence and serious cost cutting at every turn. No more than just a few hours after the failure, Venus became a brutal, horrific death planet. 99% of the people living there died a slow and extremely painful death."

"Not so long after the destruction of almost all biological life on Venus, the government sent condolences to the bereaved families of the deceased on Earth, Mars and the Moon, but offered no compensation at all. The reactor on

Venus was put right in the end and within ten years Venus was a place that could sustain human life once again."

"Now of course, people were extremely hesitant at first, but in time they did inhabit Venus again and still do to the year 2775, after which, I have no further information. From the things I heard though, most of the people on Venus preferred life there as opposed to earth, as earth is complete mess in 2775, well what's left of it anyway."

"Not long after humans re-inhabited Venus again, an organisation that became known as LINGER appears, seemingly from out of nowhere, though there are rumours that they have been going for hundreds of years, hidden somewhere beneath the surface of the earth. LINGER was and still is, controlled by a man they call 'the Director,' he is said to have come up with the FTL idea, and set about assigning various tasks to the workers and agents within the organisation to realise his FTL dreams."

"When we started working on the project, we all thought it was for a good cause, not until Winston, my mentor and guide at the time, who had originally brought me into all of this from my original timeline, much like I did with you, explained that he had a bad feeling about this project, but couldn't place his hand on what exactly it was. It wasn't until Winston had the misfortune of meeting with the Director, he finally got a more of a valid reason to try and stop his vision. He discovered the Director isn't using this FTL project just as a medium to travel faster than light across the galaxy, but he wants to use it as a weapon to destroy the colonised planets in a blink of an eye. There are many reasons floating around as to why the Director has become a psychopath, wants to destroy everything the human race has worked so hard to achieve and kill millions in the process. The main one being that it's his form of revenge on the government, revenge on the universe. He had family that were among the people wiped out on the failed colonisation attempt on Venus, and his grandfather is the brilliant man who got this all started and was cast aside and left to be forgotten."

"So, there you go, for now you are mostly up to date, but I think that's more than enough information for you right now." Zee stood up and walked over to where Edith was sitting and picked up another cup of tea.

"Zee, this is a lot to take in for me you know? I need a little time to try and digest all that."

"Sure, it will all sink in for you soon enough." Zee said, slurping his tea.

"So, what is our next move?" I asked, while giving my sore head a gentle rub.

"Next move? We stop them of course!" Zee shrugged, as if it was nothing, spilling his tea all over an expensive looking rug.

"Ok, but how?" I asked.

Zee placed his cup back down on the table next to Edith, who unbelievably didn't seem to react at all to our conversation, then made his way back over to the bed. "By retrieving an object needed to complete their project before they do of course. They may have the terbimanium, but trust me, they ain't got this one yet." He then reached down and picked up the suitcase and laid it back on the bed, clicking it open once more.

"This should do." He pulled out an itchy looking black suit and a pair of extremely shiny brown shoes.

"And who is that for?"

"It's clearly for you Charlie." He flung the clothes at me, which I caught with ease. Then he placed the shoes on the floor next to my feet. "We are going to go for a little walk. I don't want you attracting any unwanted attention. Not many people in the south of England in 1912 went around dressed as an ancient Spartan."

"Oh, yeah, right." I looked down at myself, of course I was still wearing the Spartan tunic.

"I'll be outside waiting." He took his suitcase, whispered something to Edith, who fluttered her eyelids, bushing, then grabbed a suit jacket and a coat which was hanging on a rail close to the front door. He put the jacket on and swung the coat over his shoulder and left through the main door.

"Quick as you can Charlie". Zee said as he left the tiny flat, leaving the door open.

I made my way to the bathroom as fast as my now minor headache would allow me and changed into the black suit, yup, Itchy. It felt a little clingy, suits have never really been my thing. I wondered how I was ever fine with it TBWA. I folded up the tunic and left the bathroom looking for somewhere to put it.

"You can leave it on the bed. Your twin said he would come back for it." Edith said, sipping more tea.

My twin, really? Way to go Zee.

I thanked Edith for everything as I finished doing up my shiny shoes and left the flat.

"How do I look?" I asked Zee, who was outside kicking some kind of can around the street.

"Much better than the first time I saw you." He stifled a laugh.

"Ha-ha. Funny," We began walking down a narrow cobbled street. There was a wonderful refreshing breeze that seemed to give me a new lease of life.

"The kronometers we have on us now are trackable, LINGER will know I've used them and considering we are not going back to the moon-base, they will correctly assume I've gone off to find something very important that they need. So we will only have a limited time before they track them and come looking for us." Zee rubbed his hands together and began to blow into them.

"I think I have bought us a little bit of extra time since I helped them get terbimanium. They are currently convinced that I've gone to return you back to your timeline. So we should still have a few more days to get the object before they show up again." Zee shuddered in the cold. "Oof, it's chilly here right?"

It got chillier. I tightened my jacket around me as we kept on walking down the street.

"So what is this object we need this time anyway?" I asked, fearing the worst.

"Thankfully, the item we need is small, it should fit in a pocket. The trick is to find the dammed thing. Luckily, I know exactly where to look."

"Great! Where?"

Zee smiled as we took a sharp turn around the corner. I looked up to see a gigantic ship with the name T I T A N I C written in large yellow letters on its hull.

ELEVEN

AD 1912 - April 10 - Charlie

"Tickets please." The uniformed man at the top of the ramp leading into the massive ship seemed flustered, slightly displeased and subtly rude. Zee nodded to him and pulled out two first class tickets from his inside jacket pocket and handed them over to him.

"Here you go my good man, two tickets, one for myself and one for my much older looking brother." Zee gave a charming smile. I could see how excited he was to board this iconic masterpiece, as was I, though knowing the fate of this monster did make me feel uneasy.

The crew member took the tickets and had a good look at them, then looked up at the both of us. "First class, very good gentlemen, do you have any luggage my porter can help with?" He asked politely, with a fake smile planted on his face.

"No, thank you, we are all set. This is all we came with."

Zee lifted up the suitcase as if to assume the man was incapable of looking down at it.

"Welcome aboard then sirs, the porter here will show you the way to your suite."

We stepped inside one of the most famous ships in human history. Adrenaline rushed though my entire body."My gosh, I'm actually on the Titanic! This is insane" I could barely contain my excitement. "Gotta say though Zee, as your older brother." I gave him a wry smile. "I wish there was something we could do to at least warn these poor people of the fate of this ship."

"I know Charlie, it's pretty exciting isn't it, but we can't change the outcome of this journey. Try and think of it as if it has already happened, we are just on the Titanic theme park ride, a really realistic one!" Zee smiled, as we trailed closely behind the porter on the way to our suite.

"Should I ask where you managed to obtain these tickets Zee?" I asked sceptically.

"Won 'em in a game of poker in the pub by the docks." Zee gave me a wink.

"Right. "I rolled my eyes. "I won't ask then."

After climbing three sets of metal stars, I was still in awe of my surroundings. This is actually the Titanic, the real Titanic. I always had an interest the story of this ship, but to actually walk around inside it was mind blowing. Finally, we arrived at our suite, E-202. Upon entering the suite, I was struck by the intricate detail of the room. There were several wall lamps on all four walls, an amazing Persian style carpet that had clearly never been walked on. There was a circular table in the middle of the room surrounded by wingback chairs, and even a fireplace! I immediately made myself at home on the large soft couch in the corner of the room, while Zee dumped his case on one of the two beds and headed off though a doorway into the bathroom.

"Woah. Charlie! Come check this out. They've got standard WC here! And a shower too." Zee called from inside in bathroom.

"Yea, I know." I pulled off my shoes and flopped down on the couch, placed my legs on the finely sculpted wooden table, with both hands behind my head and stared at the shimmering crystal chandelier.

"So. What exactly are we looking for?" Attempting to remind Zee of the sole purpose of why we are here.

"It's a gem." Zee said. "A blue gem, that was cut into a

necklace some time in the past. Apparently it was part of an asteroid that came down thousands of years ago somewhere in the Greenland area."

"Wait, what? Are you telling saying we are looking for the freaking 'Heart of the Ocean' necklace?! The one Rose was gifted by her fiancé in the movie Titanic?" He had to be pulling my leg.

"I know, my guess is that the guys who made that movie must have done their research well. While there is a priceless necklace onboard this ship it is not called 'The Heart of the Ocean,' at least not as far as I'm aware. That's just a dumb name that the writers chose to give it. Also, Rose and whoever, obviously are just fictional characters put in the movie to give the film something other than 'A big boat sinks' — the end." Zee said as he walked back out from the bathroom drying his face with a towel.

"Okay. So, who owns this necklace? How on earth are we going to find a tiny necklace on a ship this size?" I asked.

"I don't know exactly, searching is a good start I suppose and it ain't that tiny." Zee shrugged, flinging himself sideways down on his bed.

"I think the ship sets sail at noon. Let's go out to the main deck and wave off to the all the people on the dock." I said to Zee, who seemed to be busy checking out every nook and cranny of the room.

"Yeah good idea! What's the time now?" He said, turning back to me. I could hear the excitement in his voice as I pulled up my sleeve to check the time on my kronometer.

"11:46am." I replied.

"Well, let's go then, let's go see some history." He said as he pushing my leg off the table and flicking my ear.

"Jesus Zee, What are you? Five?" I shouted as he disappeared through the suite door.

On the deck there must have been thousands of people, from all walks of life, all of them hanging over the railings of the ship waving frantically and cheering at the people on the docks, who were equally doing the same thing right back.

If only they knew, I thought. If only they knew.

At exactly, twelve noon, the ships' horn gave a loud blast while black smoke simultaneously came bellowing out from the four gigantic funnels lining the top of the ship.

I looked over at Zee and noticed he had a ridiculously fake look of sadness about him.

"You ok Zee?" I couldn't tell if this was real, or he was playing some kind of game.

"Look at all these people Charlie. I don't think I've ever had so many people who are going to miss me this much." He said glumly, with a smirk on his face at the same time, as the ship slowly moved further into the sea and the sounds of the cheers began to fade away. I had to give a little laugh, because for just a moment, I was a little bit proud that this guy was actually me.

"Hey, you know there's a party for the first class passengers tonight at 7pm in the main hall. We should go, at least to meet some of the other passengers. Maybe we could find some more information as to where this asteroid might be hiding." Zee said with excitement laced in his voice.

"I'm in!" The thought of going to a first class party about the infamous Titanic was enough to make me feel a little giddy.

***

The party was in full swing as Zee and I sat down at a

table in the corner of a large hall in the hope that we might spot someone, or something that might give us a clue as to the whereabouts of this necklace. In the background, the titanic orchestra was playing soft classical music. This wasn't your regular, everyday party, which reeked of booze, sweat and cheap cigarettes. It was a far more luxurious affair, where obviously the rich came to play the 'I'm richer than you game'.

"Hey Zee," I leant over to him so as not to let anyone else accidentally overhear what I was about to say. "When does this ship hit the iceberg? Can you remember?"

"It's early morning of April 15 I believe, around midnight." Why do you ask?

"Just checking how much time we have left to find the necklace that's all. Four whole days sounds like a lot but this is a bloody big ship!" I helped myself to another glass of champagne from the waiter's tray as he passed by our table.

"You might want to slow down on your alcohol intake mate, we need to keep a clear head." Zee said, as he sipped on the first and only glass he'd have all evening. "You stank of the stuff when I brought you out of Sparta, probably made it much easier for me to sneak up behind you."

"I'm perfectly fine, I'm just getting into the moment is all." I lied.

"Ok, listen, while I have it in the front of my mind, set your Kronometer to 1832, New Salem, Illinois, that is going to be our next stop. There could be a very good chance we get split up on this boat and I need to make sure we wind up in the same place. So when the time comes, hit that button ok."

"OK, sure, any particular reason we might be going to New Salem after this?" I asked, while setting the kronometer to the exact time and place Zee had asked me to.

He looked away from me, towards the crowd of people at the other side of the room. "You don't need to know that yet Charlie. Just concentrate on finding the necklace ok."

The party came and went without Zee and I finding out a single thing about the potential whereabouts of this gem.

***

* * *

Before we knew it, four whole days had passed by in what seemed like mere seconds. We got to know a few of the other passengers in first class, but they were too interested in themselves and their money to even bother to answer any questions we might have. Needless to say, there was still no sign of this necklace and we had spent as much time as we was humanly possible, wandering around the ship, analysing people, looking for any kind of clue. Still, Zee remained remarkably calm, but I was beginning to get increasingly anxious that we were going to fail this mission too. Not to mention my new knowledge that these kronometers can be tracked by LINGER

To be fair, we had a great time during the past four days. We both visited the ship's barber and bagged ourselves a classic early twentieth century haircut. We entered into a shuffleboard tournament, which was something I had heard of, but never actually got a chance to play. It was just like darts or archery, but involving a shuffleboard table that was long and made of very slippy polished wood. It gives you the chance to aim and shoot small coloured pucks at areas marked on the board, with hopes of scoring one, two, three or four points. Only the winner scores in each round, so you have to play wisely. I even took the time to visit the onboard swimming pool, not only to try and scope out this necklace, but because I wanted to see the first swimming pool ever built onboard a ship and it turns out it was heated! However, I was now beginning to wonder if the gem even existed at all. We only had few hours until the Titanic was due to hit an iceberg.

Zee and I sat together in silence at a dinner table, clueless and devoid of all ideas on what to do. It felt like we had failed again.

"Sheesh, I should have known this would be worse than finding a needle in a floating haystack." Zee said as he slouched back into his dining chair. He still didn't seem to be as concerned as I would have expected.

I sat in silence, gazing out into the huge dining area. Staring at it nothing really, just looking out there, blankly. My eyes wandered over to a group of women all wearing long white frilly dresses and gigantic colourful hats.

"Zee, what colour did you say this gem is again?"

"It's blue. Well, like a purpley bluey colour, why?"

I slowly raised my hand up over the table and extended my index finger even slower. I could feel my eyes widening. "There! My G— It's th—." I shot up out of my seat, knocking my chair over backwards behind me.

"Shhtp! Charlie, sit down!" Zee grabbed my shoulder, quickly retrieved my chair and sat me back down on it. "Where? Show me. What can you see?"

I held my mouth tightly shut, while thrusting my index finger in the direction of the young lady sitting alone on a table in the middle of the room, my eyes still trying their hardest to pop out of my head.

Zee leaned over towards me and cocked his head in the direction I was pointing. "My god, Charlie that's it! You've found it."

"How do we get it?" I asked, eager to just run over and grab it.

"Ok, Let's think". Zee stroked his invisible beard still fixated on the necklace. "We should go over there." He concluded.

"Right, obviously. How?"

"Well, I guess we just get up and go over and ask if we can join her." Zee's nerves clearly rising to the surface.

"Join her? What just like that? Out of the blue? She's definitely going to think we are up to something."

Zee looked at me as if I was a complete fool." Well, aren't

we?"

As if by the most perfect timing the universe could possibly muster. It was at this exact moment in time that two men walked over to her table and sat in front of her, both of them smiling like they had just won the lottery.

"SHIT! It's Colonel Fone!" Zee shouted, he was almost hysterical.

"Shhtp Zee! You are as bad as I am. Who the hell is Colonel Fone?" I asked, holding my hand over his mouth now, while struggling to get a better look at his face from this distance." Is he a LINGER agent? And who's the other guy with him?"

"You bet your arse he is." Zee said, removing my hand from his face. "Angry, grumpy and insanely stupid. I gotta say though, I don't recognise the other guy, I can only assume that he is an agent too. They must have tracked us and more than likely figured out what we are looking for." Zee spoke frantically. We both looked at each other, knowing exactly what we needed to do.

***

* * *

The young woman wearing the necklace looked up at us as we approached. The two agents were facing away from us and hadn't noticed we were there yet.

"Why good evening Colonel Fone," Zee said to the Colonel, who was completely caught off guard and froze for a moment, then turned to the young woman sitting opposite the two agents. "My lady, I don't believe we have had the pleasure of meeting. My name is Jaques." Zee cleared his throat as he spoke. "Jaques Kitteredge."

"Rosaline." She answered politely offering her hand. "A pleasure."

"Rosaline, well, what do you know? That's a name I didn't expect to hear on board this ship." Zee said, looking at me and raising a brow. "Anyway, I don't suppose we could borrow your salt at all could we? Ours seems to have gone missing from our table. Probably been swooped up in the loops of time somewhere I should imagine hey." He pointed at the salt on the table just across from the agents, while resting his hand on Colonel Fone's shoulder.

Colonel Fone, who had now awakened from his stupor of surprise, decided that he would oblige in our request. "Oh, yes of course. Let me jus— Zee!" He stood up to face Zee and caught a look at me, then turned his gaze back to Zee. "The Director informs you are returning your original self back to his original timeline. Are we off course slightly?"

"Oh my, you didn't tell me that you were a Colonel." The young woman began. "My great uncle is in the army, are you in th—?"

"Yes, yes we are." The other agent said, cutting her off.

Colonel Fone continued. "Zee," he leaned in towards Zee's face. Closer than I would imagine conformable for anyone. "You would be wise to do as the Director directs."

"Well, yes the Director does direct, and I am certainly wise to do indeed." I could see Zee liked to have fun with this guy.

"What? Yes! That is what I said isn't it?" Colonel Fone seemed to be quickly sinking into a world of confusion.

"No, it isn't what you said." Zee replied confidently.

Just as the other agent began to stand up from his chair, presumably to try and resolve the issue of Colonel Fone being incessantly teased and belittled by Zee, there was a violent shudder. The Titanic suddenly lurched sideways, briefly throwing people off balance. The room fell totally silent for a moment as the people around us tried to comprehend what had just happened.

Myself, Zee, Colonel Fone and the other agent all knew very well what had just happened. I checked the time on my kronometer, 11:42pm, the history books seemed to have gotten this one pretty much spot on. I took a moment to glance at the other three men. Zee was holding on to the back of a chair. Colonel Fone had grabbed hold of his compatriots arm in fright, who was in turn trying to calm the Colonel down and simultaneously explain to the young woman that there was nothing to worry about.

"Its ok, He just doesn't like sinking ships." He was frantically trying to peel Colonel Fone's hands off his arm.

"The ship is sinking!?" The young woman shouted, alerting the entire room of this fact. Panic ensued. It has to be now I thought.

I used Zee as leverage, and quickly flung myself over the table towards Rosaline. "I bet this one isn't in the history books." I muttered as I swung my arm towards the necklace and tore it from her neck. Thankfully the chain snapped easily and I found myself holding the large blue gem in my hand as adrenaline began rapidly pumping around my entire body.

"Run Zee!" I called, setting my legs into action.

I took off in the direction of the white swing-doors at the far end of the hall, gripping the rock so tightly it was making my fingers ache.

"My Diamond! My Diamond!" I could hear Rosaline's screams far clearer than any of the panic shouts and cries from the other passengers in the room.

"Right behind you Charlie. Just go!" I could feel Zee's hand pushing against my back.

I turned around to see Zee right behind me, his eyes wide, his lips pursed. Just beyond him, I could see the two agents giving chase. We began jumping over the tables and pushing away chairs to try and create any kind of barrier between us and the agents. We crashed through the main doors of the hall and sprinted up the grand staircase, down a long corridor and finally to an opening that lead to the outside decking.

"Charlie wait," Zee called from just behind me. "Stop here Charlie." He crouched into a small crevice by one of the lifeboats.

We both ducked into a tiny gap between the ships huge steel beams on the main deck out of sight. I proceeded to have major deja-vu episode of the alleyway outside my flat in London.

"Ok, Charlie, I think we are clear of them for now. We have to make sure our Kronometers are set for 1832, New Salem, Illinois on this date ok." His hands shaking wildly as he began fumbling around with his kronometer. "Hang on to that gem. We're almost there."

I punched in today's date for 1832, New Salem, Illinois into my device.

"Ok done. Ready Charlie? Let's get out of here!" Zee said, his breathing now begging to clam.

"Ready as I'll ever be." I said looking around trying to see if we had been tailed.

"Five, four, three, two—"

Colonel Fone grabbed me around the neck and had me in a strong choke hold before I could press the jump button on my kronometer. Feeling the breath disappear from me, I dropped the gem on the deck floor. I could hear it hit the floor with a clink and roll away in some other direction.

"Charlie!" Zee jumped at Colonel Fone like a rabid dog, throwing us all to the floor. It was time to put my non-existent martial arts skill into use. Good thing I attended a karate class when I was about eight years old. As we hit the deck, I span my body around, releasing myself from the Colonels sweaty grip, while Zee continued to wrestle on the floor with him.

"The gem Charlie! Get the gem, I've got him" Zee somehow managed to get the words out a split second before Fone had gotten up and given him a swift kick in the chest and Zee fell backwards with huge force. I span around searching frantically around the deck for the little blue gem. There, there it was, wedged in between two small divots in a small dusty corner. I dived into it, grabbed the gem and still trying to catch my breath from the headlock earlier, ran as fast as I could manage towards the front of the ship with Colonel Fone hot on my heels.

I found myself running faster than I usually could before realising that the ship was actually tilting forwards and I was actually running downhill.

"You've nowhere to go kid" Colonel Fone shouted behind me. It felt like he was only yards behind.

Seconds later, I realised that the Colonel was right. I had run right to the front of the ship and there was indeed, nowhere to go, except down into the freezing cold water. I thought about jumping and pressing the kronometer at the same time, but I just couldn't leave Zee. What if Fone had seriously hurt him? Or worse, somehow, I had to know.

I stopped dead at the front rails of this ship and span around to face the Colonel. He had stopped about five yards in front of me, starring at me, smiling. My god he wasn't even out of breath!

"Don't get any funny ideas kid." Fone edged closer to me with one hand extended and the other hovering over his holstered weapon. "Hand it over, and you won't end up dead. My colleague will be here at any moment. So you have no choice but to hand over that gem."

"Where's Zee?" I asked, feeling water beginning to lap against my feet. As the water approached him, he looked down and began to shuffle backwards away from it, just as Zee came running towards us with his finger over his mouth telling me to keep his presence a nice surprise. I pulled everything I had into not showing any kind of emotion at the sight of Zee.

"Ok Ok Colonel," I said submissively. "It's yours." I stared down at the gem and back up at Colonel Fone.

Zee was inches from his target by now, when he dived at Colonel Fone's left arm and ripped off his kronometer and backed himself away.

"What the!" The surprised Colonel wasn't entirely sure what had just happened.

Zee was holding up the kronometer and keeping his eyes firmly on Fone. "Now who doesn't have any choices?" Zee smiled, dangling the device just over the edge of the ship.

"Zee! Hey, come on man. We can make a deal here. You know I wasn't ever going to hurt anyone right?" Fone said, begging.

"You're right" Zee said. "You weren't." With that, he turned and threw the kronometer as far out to sea as he could. Which was pretty damn far.

"Nooooo!" Colonel Fone shouted and ran as fast as he could, splashing through the cold water around him and diving straight into the icy ocean towards his slowly sinking kronometer. Wails of "I can't stay here, I need to get home," were growing more and more faint as he slowly vanished into the cold darkness. There was still not a single sign of the other agent anywhere.

Zee waved his hand to beckon me over towards him" Come Charlie, we need to move back towards the stern of the ship. The bow is about to go under."

As we made our way uphill towards the stern, the ship began to creak and groan louder and louder, drowning out the chaos going on around us. We could hear the orchestra playing soft music in a commendable attempt to try and calm the passengers as women and children were lifted into lifeboats. Just as we passed the halfway point the Titanic gave out ear-splitting cracking sound and began to split itself into two. The ship opened up just a few feet from us revealing floor after floor of destruction and chaos. Thankfully, it was our side of the ship that then plunged downwards back towards the ocean sending Zee and I crashing into the railings on the outside of the ship.

"Charlie! Grab on, She's going to rise up again. I'll come to you." Zee screamed at me as he made his way over to the railing which was becoming more and more hard to hold onto.

"Don't let go! When the ship is vertical, press the jump button!"

I could feel the ship was now slowly sinking further and further into the cold dark waters of the North Atlantic sea. We were now standing on the railings next to each other.

"Now!" Zee screamed.

I could feel the sea rising swiftly over my body making me

wince in pain, then darkness.

TWELVE

AD 1832 - April 14 - Charlie

"AAHH! Am I dead?" I shrieked, while patting and prodding myself all over. "My god! That was one hell of a jump!" I exclaimed, just as the vortex spat us out onto some cool dry ground.

"Woo! Yea it was! Always a rush to leave a jump to the last second hey Charlie?" Zee was pumping the air trying to expel some obvious excess adrenaline. "Also, you're immortal mate, you can't die, remember?"

"I do remember, but as immortals, what if we *had* been swallowed up by the deadly cold waters of the North Atlantic Ocean?" I said, almost knowing what he was going to say.

"Oh yeah, that's a nasty thought. I guess we would be extremely uncomfortable for a very very long time, but not dead." Zee said with a smile."Anyway, we're over that business now, mission accomplished. We are now in 1832, good old New Salem, Illinois, where technically, the Titanic hasn't even been thought of yet. Bit weird thinking about things like that, so I usually try not to."

"You can say that again Zee!" I said. "I mean look at us. We are still wet from being on a sinking ship that doesn't even exist yet. Yeah, my head is spinning." I ruffled my hair, trying to remove the mind warping thought.

"You still got that gem, Charlie?" Zee said, turning to point at me. "Can I grab it off you please?"

"I have it yeah, here you go." I said, handing it over to him. Zee gave it a quick glance over and then placed the gem into his outside pocket.

"So, shall we?" Zee said, giving a rather dramatic bow and swayed his hand towards the direction of a small dirt road.

"Right after you mon ami." I said, playing along, attempting my best French accent, which was somewhere between bloody awful and pretty bad, only to earn a quizzical look from Zee, then we both burst out laughing and carried on walking along the dirt road.

It was a warm and sunny day in New Salem, there were dry leaves strewn all over the road and we could hear the playful yells and screams of young children nearby. I figured there must be some kind of school or nursery close to here. This place was so peaceful and quiet, the polar opposite to the carnage we had just experienced and was the perfect weather for drying off our salty wet clothes.

"So are we here to find some other material? Please say no." I asked as we passed by a row of wooden houses.

"Well, you'll be pleased to know that we are not here to find anything at all. This is just a place I come to think, whenever I need to take a break off time jumping adventures. I came across it completely by accident and I come back over and over just because its lovely here." Zee spoke with a broad smile on his face. "Also, for some reason or other, this is one of the only places in time and space that the Black Knight can't seem to track me at all."

"The what Knight?" I said, wondering if he may have been talking about some strange LINGER related medieval agent or something.

"The Black Knight Satellite, I mentioned it to you back in the flat when I picked you up. Remember?"

I thought for a moment. Wow, that really did seem like a lifetime ago.

"Ah yes! I think I remember now. Isn't that the Satellite

they use to track and communicate through time right?"

Zee put his hand on my shoulder as we walked. "Yep, but it actually does a heck of a lot more than that. Firstly, without the Black Knight your kronometer wouldn't work very well. I mean it would still work but that satellite provides the pin point accuracy of the exact time and place you want to go to. Also, fun fact, it's been in orbit for over thirteen thousand years." He looked at me and raised an eyebrow.

"What?! How on earth has it been up there for that long? Weren't people back then just figuring out how to build houses out of stone? How could they have put—"

"It was LINGER obviously Charlie. One of the first things they did when they discovered the technology to travel through time, is to travel through time, only for them to realise that they needed something more accurate to do it with. I mean, at one point they were trying to send people back to the middle ages in France, only to find they had actually been sent to New York in the 1930s. So they developed the Black Knight, put it up in orbit and sent it back through time as far as they could. Now they could go anywhere anytime with supreme accuracy, knowing it will always be there." He kicked up some dust as we walked.

"Except for some odd reason, it doesn't seem to have any tracking data for New Salem, Illinois in 1832, go figure."

After a few more minutes of walking in relative silence, we found ourselves at a quaint little place that looked like a grocery store mixed up with some kind of bar or pub.

"Ah, here we are, this is us." Zee pointed to the small building that had a small wooden sign above the door that read 'The Berry and Lincoln'.

Zee knocked on the door then immediately gave it a little shove. The door decided to announce our arrival with loud squeaking sound. I followed Zee as casually as I could into the building.

"It's high time I oiled that door. That confounded squeaking noise is fast becoming unbearable." Came a low pitched voice from behind the counter.

"Saves you the hassle of having to install an entry bell though hey Bram?" Zee said walking towards the bar.

The man was furiously cleaning some already sparkling glasses with a filthy looking towel when he turned to face us. "Zee! It's been too long my old friend." He moved swiftly around the bar to give zee handshake and a hug. He looked to be in his twenties with a remarkable stovepipe hat placed on top his head. "I see you are still sticking with that ridiculous British accent huh. That's going to get you into some trouble around here one day you know." The man gave a slight chuckle.

"Let's hope not, so far this is the *only* place I've managed to stay out of any trouble." Zee said, hugging vigorously in return. "Hey Bram, I'd like to introduce you to me, er my old buddy Charlie."

Letting go of Zee, the man turned to face me with a broad smile."Pleased to meet you Charlie, the names Lincoln, Abraham Lincoln."

"Abraham Lincoln?" I asked the younger looking Lincoln, who was beardless, making his big ears really obvious. "As in, *the* Abraham Lincoln?"

"Wh—I don't see any other Abraham Lincolns' around here, so yes, I guess I am! The one and only," he laughed, looking around the room for another Abraham Lincoln. "Let me hazard a tiny guess, you also are from the future, huh?"

"Uhm." I looked at Zee, who gave me an approving nod. "Actually yes I am from your future, we are also one and the same person too." I gestured towards Zee. "He, is me and I am him."

Abraham appeared to freeze in time for a moment before looking at Zee, then back to me and back to Zee again before bursting out laughing. "My, you boys are hilariously absurd!" He continued to laugh as he turned back towards the bar. "Come on my boys, over this way, let me get you both a drink. The entertainment you provide makes it more than worthy of being on the house." He showed us to couple of stools at the bar. "Beer or brandy?" Abraham called out as he walked around to the other side of the bar.

"Thanks Abe. I'll have a Brandy please." Zee replied.

"How about you, uhm, uh—"

"Charlie," I finished the sentence up for him, "I'll take a beer if that's ok. Thank you."

"Ah yes, Charlie, I'll remember that." Abraham turned, fumbled around, turned back to face us some seconds later with two bottles of beer and a glass of brandy. He placed the glass in front of Zee, a bottle of beer for me and another beer for himself. Then he took a seat behind the bar directly in front of us and raised his bottle up towards Zee. "Cheers Zee, I must say it's great to see you again, and as a bonus for me, I get to see you twice!" He turned to look at me and clinked his bottle against mine.

"So, I heard there was some sort of local election around here. Did you give one of your dazzling speeches again?" Zee started, after a sip of his brandy.

"Ahh indeed there was, I bagged myself enough votes to earn myself an all time best — sixth place! " He laughed and took a swig of beer. "You see Zee, my proposed policies are short and sweet and very much to the point, much like an old woman's dance routine." Abraham raised his arms and slowly lowered them down to his sides as if to mimic some kind of dance.

"I hope you didn't actually say that in your speech Abe!" Zee said looking at Abraham Lincoln with wide eyes. "You didn't publicly compare your policies to an old lady did you?"

"I most certainly did my boy. I most certainly did." He turned to the side and gave Zee a subtle wink as they both burst into laughter leaving me utterly lost, drinking from my bottle slowly and quietly.

"So myself and the Whigs completely lost the election. But rather than letting that get me down and fuel an inner desire to give it all up, quite the opposite has happened. It has given me some enthusiasm for politics like I never before experienced, quite something I must say. I've come to realise that my most prioritised aim is to preserve the Union at all costs. For me, it is the most important thing we can achieve, along of course with abolishing the wretched legalities of one human being owning another human being. The abolition of slavery and the saviour of the Union, which is at one with bringing a democratic government to the people of this Great united Nation of ours." He was standing tall behind the bar as if he was giving another one of his infamous speeches.

I found myself in awe of this mans' charisma and to think that in a short period of time from now he pretty much fulfilled all of what he had just said. We all seemed to be lost in our thoughts for a moment, when for some inexplicable reason there was a loud bang on the bar.

"Jesus Zee! You scared the bloody daylights out of me." I said as I held on to my fast beating chest. Zee chuckled as he used his other hand to free the blue gem from the surrounding diamonds and from the necklace itself. Zee then put the gem back into his pocket and gathered up the remaining diamonds into a nice neat pile in front of Abe.

"Abe, I heard of the tragic loss of your business partner and good friend, Bill. I'm really sorry." Zee said sympathetically.

Abraham sighed. "Mmm, his death came as a shock to all of us." He suddenly sounded really sad. "May William Franklin Berry's soul keep resting in eternal peace." He raised his bottle to the ceiling, then took a small sip and returned it back to the bar.

"I want you to take these diamonds Abe," Zee said, sliding them over towards Abraham. "I know you've had to spend a lot of money since Bills death, so you should use this to pay off some of the debts you might have. Should have a fair bit left over once you have too."

"Oh my! You really didn't have—." Abraham began.

"It's fine Abe." Zee interrupted, giving Abe a gentle pat on his shoulder. "Take it, please."

Abe stopped and stared deeply at the diamonds gleaming and glistening in his palm, then back at Zee. "I have finally found myself with no words. Thank you Zee. Thank you."

"You know Charlie," Zee said, turning to me, "Abe here, is a true example of the phrase *jack of all trades*." We all laughed, lightening up the mood again, probably Zee's way of not letting me feel left out of the conversation, which to be fair, was becoming a little intense. "It's true though, I mean get this, he has been a boatman, a soldier during the black hawk war, a postmaster, surveyor, rail splitter, a general store owner, and now" Zee took a pause and looked at Abe, "an aspiring President of the United States."

"Hah! Don't be ridiculous Zee." Abraham laughed. "That's rather farfetched wouldn't you say?"

"Well, maybe. But till then Abe, till then." Zee gulped down the remaining contents of his glass.

"May I offer you gentlemen a refill?" Abraham asked, as he stood up from his seat.

"Nah, I'm good thanks Abe." Zee said, pushing his glass over towards him.

"Of course, if you say so." Abe said, pausing for a moment. "My fine sirs, if I may, I'll leave you both to your business as I have some very pressing business of my own to attend to. Please help yourselves to anything behind the bar as you wish." Abraham said, standing to his feet. "Zee, Charlie, thank you so much for your time and amazing generosity, of which one day I hope I can repay." Abraham said gratefully, then disappeared through a door behind the counter.

"Wow, that guy is something else hey. So, what's next for us immortal, time-travelling super adventurers?" I asked Zee as we were left alone at the bar.

Zee leaned back into his chair and sighed, then came back up, almost immediately. "Well, I don't know exactly how to tell you this mate, trust me I've been meaning too for a while now and it won't be easy for you to hear either, but you still need to know anyway. You need to know for the good of the future of this planet and possibly the entire universe."

"Ok, you need me to know something that could decide the fate of the entire universe? Well, this sounds kinda bad, What is it?" I tried and obviously completely failed to prepare my mind for anything coming my way.

"Well, to try to put this information into its most basic form, we, that is you and me, are father, or fathers, if you want to be technical about it, of the founder of LINGER"

I stared motionless at Zee, blinking slowly and taking some seconds to process the information I'd just been given before replying. "Ok what's that now? I don't get it. Firstly, doesn't the immortality serum make us completely infertile anyway? So how on earth can we be biological fathers?" I stated.

Zee just smiled. "No matter how hard you try, you can't change the past Charlie."

"Yes, this has been said before Zee. Care to explain what on earth is going on here for me please? Are you seriously saying that we are responsible for all this mess?" I felt the panic rising up into my brain.

"Well, the Director, is of our birth lineage yes. The son of one of the brightest minds ever to live whose terraforming idea was stolen by the government. That man's mind belonged to our son Charlie, our son."

"Zee, just backup for a second here will you. I thought you said earlier, that the terraforming was completed around the year 2745. I mean, how is that possible when my natural timeline is as far back as 2019. Unless it was him who created the serum. But that still doesn't make sense, because the serum makes one immortal. I'm extremely lost Zee, help me out here." I said rapidly, more panic being injected into to mind.

"Ok, relax, sit comfortably and let me try and explain it. In the year 2063, a man called Nathan Anderson was awarded a contract to aid spaceX with the terraforming plan of Mars, as he was noted to be one of the brightest minds alive at the time. If you remember I told you his work on terraforming human habitation techniques and the pure science of other worldly colonisation was stolen and no credit whatsoever was given to him. At around this time he also had a son, a young boy by the name Gareth who was in some ways far smarter than his father. Gareth learned of his fathers betrayal and when he was old enough he decided he needed to keep his fathers' work alive. He also tried fighting the government to get the credit owed to his father reinstated, but failed. It was around this time that Gareth vanished, no one saw or heard from him again for a long long time. In secret and in a perfect storm of rage, hatred and super intelligence, he created a serum that would keep alive him for a longer time. As it turns out, it made him pretty much immortal, though he did still show signs of ageing, it wasn't anything anyone would notice in their entire lifetimes. Now, and this is a little bit of speculation, but at some point, maybe a few hundred years later, having gone quite mad, he concentrated on making an army of his own, an army that would in time crush the corrupt governments and attempt to control everything and everywhere humans had colonised. He created hundreds of pieces of tech that were worlds apart from anything anyone had ever seen before. In short, LINGER was born. In the year 2745 the colonising project of Venus was completed and as we know the reactor keeping air breathable failed, apparently killing the love of his life who was stationed there. This was the moment he snapped. His quest for revenge was reignited and burned with a raging fury. He doesn't only want to take his revenge on the government, but to use LINGER to gain full control over the entire solar system at any cost and this is the sole reason he is building the FTL weapon. So, Charlie, the Director is your grandson." Zee finished.

I felt like my head was going to implode under the weight of all this information. I had to stand up and hold onto something to keep me from passing out, maybe never to wake up again. I began to frantically pace up and down the bar mumbling something that even I had no idea what.

"I'm sorry I dragged you into all this, Charlie. I know that I've ruined the life you had, but I felt that you would understand and see the bigger picture. I had no choice." Zee ran his hand through his hair, clearly frustrated. "I could return you back to your timeline right now you know, so you can get back to the life you had in 2019, what's left of it anyway." He stood up and placed a kronometer in front of me. "One more jump left in this one. "

I picked up the device and held on to it tightly. How could

I just go back to my old life knowing what I know now? How could I leave Zee to fight this fight which is just as much my fight as his?

"No," I pushed the kronometer back towards Zee. "We have the gem, the upper hand. Let's do what we need to do to save the universe from this madman."

Zee paused, smiled and extended his hand towards the kronometer. "You won't regret this Charlie!" he pocketed the kronometer and set his device for 1989, Berlin and beckoned me to do the same, then smiled.

"Let's do this" He said with a grin.

"Berlin, 1989, is this time and place somehow relevant in our mission?" I asked unable to figure out why this time and place might be important.

"Very, it's the location of the real gem." He pushed his kronometer button and vanished into a crackling spiral of plasma.

"It's the location of the rea— What?!" I pushed my button as if to chase after him so he could explain himself while we ride the rainbow vortex of doom.

THIRTEEN

AD 1989 - November 9 - Charlie

The World is too small for walls, read one slogan. *Demokratie,* read another. There were hundreds of slogans strewn all over the huge wall as we walked by. We could hear what sounded like a massive crowd building on the other side. It sounded absolutely terrifying.

"Jesus Zee, this place makes me really nervous. If my history knowledge serves me well, that wall is coming down today and hordes of 'soon to be free' people are going to be coming this way. Are we safe here?" I struggled to keep up with Zees' walking pace as he seemed to know exactly where he was headed. "Also! Are you telling me the gem in your pocket, the gem we almost died for, is a fake? And you knew it? Come on Zee, we could have been killed!"

"Yeah, that's right, I had the gem replicated by a really amazing gem cutter in Sri Lanka in 1911 who gifted it to wealthy British family who were emigrating from England to America aboard the Titanic. I figured it would be a good idea to have a duplicate in case of any unforeseen emergency or to use it as a red herring. In this case, it was the latter that came of use." Zee said, continuing his fast pace. "I didn't mean for our expedition on the Titanic to go right down to the wire like that, really I didn't. I assumed we would have found it within a day or two of being onboard."

"So, the real gem is somewhere here then? Jesus Zee it had better bloody be!" I was seething and couldn't shake the feeling that I was on some sort of wild goose chase.

"You bet it is, or at least I hope it still is anyway. I thought it a good idea to come to Berlin at this particular time for two reasons. Firstly, there is about to be absolute chaos around here, and secondly, the gem is here." Zee turned to give me a little smile.

I knew a fair bit about the history of this wall. It was as much symbolic as it was a physical deterrent. The *official* purpose was actually to keep, so-called western fascists from entering East Germany and undermining the socialist state, but then, it primarily served the objective of stemming mass defections from east to west. I also knew all too well the imminent chaos that Zee had just mentioned was indeed very real. This was a moment in history which was a huge turning point for millions of people all across Europe, especially ones from socialist regimes. It also brought the cold war to an abrupt end.

Zee stopped and turned towards the giant wall while making subtle clicking sounds with this teeth. "Somewhere here," Zee was happily talking to himself while tapping the wall with his knuckle, presumably listening for some kind of distinct sound. Though I'm unsure how he could hear anything over the din coming from the other side, which was growing louder and closer.

"Ahh ha" Zee exclaimed as he stopped over a small area of wall that had the slogan *WHY?* Written in black spray paint. He took two steps backwards away from the wall and was standing directly over a small circular manhole. "This is it Charlie." Zee said, looking at me with a finger pointing downwards.

"Is it?" I asked, not knowing what *it* was in the slightest.

Zee began to pry open the edge of the manhole cover with a stick he'd found at the base of the wall. "Follow me quickly." He pulled off his backpack, threw it down the now open and pitch black hole, then lowered himself in.

With his hands placed on the edge of the gap, he looked up and me and winked. "Gernonimo!" Down he went.

Well, this is a little less glamorous I thought to myself. I hate small dark spaces, why on earth would I have hidden something so important down there? I shook my head, shrugging off the thoughts of being eaten by giant radioactive rats, or drowning in god knows what. I gently lowered myself into the hole, it was absolutely pitch dark down there.

"Lower yourself in Charlie. Make sure you pull the cover back over the hole before you let go." The sound of Zee echoed from somewhere beneath me.

I lent over the edge, dragged the cover towards me and lowered myself in while pulling it over my head. It made a terrifying screeching sound as it closed out any light there once was into none at all. "Ok, three, two and—" I let go of the edge and dropped down into the darkness. Almost as instantly I was falling, I was in the ams of Zee who was holding on to me as I landed.

"Euugh! It stinks down here!" I said, positive I was about to vomit.

"Well, duh, It's a sewer. Did you expect it to smell like

cookies fresh out of the oven?" Zee chuckled.

He pulled out a small torch from his backpack and clicked it on. "These walls are narrow and the ceiling is low, so watch your head ok. Right, let's go, follow me." He said as he bent down and began to move into the dark, stinking sewer tunnel with me following just inches behind him.

As we inched forward I got the very distinct feeling that we were going downhill. The disgusting, putrid liquid that was rising up my legs confirmed this.

"Zee this gem better be close or I swear if I chuck up, it's going all over you." I said holding my hand over as much as my nose and mouth as I could.

"Just another eight miles mate." Zee said, seemingly enjoying my suffering.

"Screw you Zee!" I knew he was joking, but I hated him all the same right now.

Finally, we arrived at small door, that was barely big enough to fit a small child through. Zee stopped, pulled off his backpack and placed it on small ledge beside the door.

"Let's go." He said, looking at me as he pushed open the slightly stiff door and squeezed himself through.

I followed right behind and immediately realised that the

floor wasn't wet anymore and the stench was far more bearable that on the other side. Ahead of me I could see Zee making his way up some narrow stairs.

"Careful, these stairs are steep and a little slippery." Zee warned as I put my foot onto the first step and immediately slipped.

"So," I started after I had found my slippery stairs rhythm. "Why did you hide the real gem in a stinking sewer underneath Berlin?" I asked, as we kept moving upwards.

"Well, obviously I wanted to hide it somewhere that no one would ever find it." Came Zee's muffled voice, due to the narrowing of the walls and the steepening of the stairs.

Reaching the top of the stairs presented us with yet another door, which was a little larger than the one at the bottom, but only just. As we entered the smell returned, but worse, way way worse.

"Jeez! What the hell!?" I grimaced and cringed my nose in disgust, using my arm as a face mask to cover my nose and mouth which was doing little to nothing to help.

"Oh yea, sorry I guess I should have warned you about this one. This is the old Soviet sewer system from back in the forties and you are now smelling fifty year old crap.

Quite the history lesson today huh."

Fair enough I thought to myself. I guess I had been riding the glamour bus recently, from setting sail aboard the Titanic to meeting with Abraham Lincoln. I guess on the balance of things, smelling fifty year old Adolf Hitler shit makes it relatively even.

My nose was just beginning to become accustomed to the smell as we arrived at a tiny hatch in the ceiling.

"Ok, we are here." Zee said, pushing the hatch upwards letting a gust of wonderful cool non foul smelling air come flooding over my face.

"Ah! Air." I said, gasping. "Please tell me this is it. Please."

Zee climbed up into the hatch, turned himself around and then pulled me up after him. "Yep, this is it Charlie. This is an old bunker that was used by Hitler during his final hours of the war. At least I think it is judging by that—." Zee pointed to a small table with a large red old style telephone on it. "And those—" He gestured towards the wall above the small table.

On the wall there were paintings of nazi soldiers, senior military officials and even one of Hitler himself, all in pristine condition. There were pens on the table, some with the lids off, open books, metallic cups with some sort of dried up black liquid inside them and the chairs were all tipped over like this place was evacuated in a massive hurry.

"This is amazing." I said, soaking in the thick atmosphere.

"Yeah, it really is, apparently there were quite a lot of high ranking military officials as well as soldiers in this place and where there are soldiers, there are weapons." He stated, while moving on through a perfectly carved wooded doorway. "Which reminds me," he pointed towards the ground close to me, "do be careful, there might be some unexploded bombs or mines, lurking around here somewhere."

"You're kidding me right?" I panicked and stared around to find if there was some kind of time bomb ticking, mine or a grenade lying around somewhere by my feet.

"You should see your face right now Charlie." He laughed out loud, his voice echoing around the bunker.

"I hope I amuse you Zee, really I do."

We rounded a tight corner and then found ourselves in a chamber of some sort. Zee switched the light on, which was still working! They really don't make them like they used to, I thought to myself, illuminating the one of the most unbelievable sights I have ever seen in my life.

"Holy Moses!" I exclaimed as my eyes adjusted to the light to see vast amounts of treasures scattered all over the floor and piled up in each corner of the room. There were gold coins, exquisite paintings and all types of jewellery from all over the world I was sure. I dreaded to think where or how the Nazis acquired all of this stuff.

"How did you, how?—" I stuttered on my words, pointing towards the hordes of valuables.

"How did I get access to the stolen Nazis treasures?" Zee finished for me. I nodded in affirmation as it was all I could manage.

"I don't know, I just did. I guess you could call it a very long story. Another time hey?" He shrugged and moved over to the far end of the room.

"That's unbelievable Zee, you don't just magically pop up on som—." I stopped mid-way through my sentence as I noticed Zee had moved over to the far end of the room where there was, what could only be described as, a pirates treasure chest pulled right out of some Disney movie. Zee carefully clicked the two metal latches on the front of the chest and opened it, revealing more coins and even more jewellery. But, what really caught my attention was the necklace he pulled out of it. The exact replica of the gem we had salvaged from the neck of the nice unsuspecting lady on the Titanic.

He held the necklace high above his head and smashed it on the hard wall, breaking the gem free, spilling diamonds all over the floor and smashing the chain into pieces.

"You're getting good at smashing that thing." I pointed out sarcastically. "How come no one knows of this treasure buried here, besides you?" I questioned again.

"Let's just say a search team, if there is one, is still yet to find this place. My guess is they believe they've searched every nook and cranny of around here and have just called it quits. You've got to admit though, the pungent stink could make one believe there is nothing but sewage waste down here anyway." Zee stood up looking closely at the gem as if he was some kind of jeweller looking for defects.

"Right! Excellent, we're done mate. Come on, let's get out of here pronto." Zee said, prying a diamond from the side of the gem and flicking it onto the floor as if it was an annoying pebble and not a priceless piece of jewellery.

The trek back out lead us back through the way we came, but thankfully it seemed far easier than on the way in. The pungent smell was also more bearable for some reason too.

Opening the man hole hatch from the inside and seeing the light stream into the darkness, made my eyes felt alive again, as was the cool crisp air that followed, filling in my lungs with so much heaven it felt amazing to be alive. As we climbed out of the hole we found ourselves right in the middle of thousands of people all shouting and cheering as large oblong chunks of the wall were being pulled down by cranes and bulldozers and crashing to the floor around us.

"Chaos!" Zee shouted, trying and make himself heard above the noise of the crowds. "This is perfect!" He grabbed my arm and gestured towards an alleyway between two large grey office blocks. "Let's get out of here."

Really all I wanted to do was to soak all of this amazing atmosphere in. I wanted to join in with the crowds of elated people seeing their freedom return to their lives once more. But Zee seemed really nervous and dragged towards the alleyway. "Charlie come on, let's go!" He was clearly disturbed by something he had either seen or heard.

"Ok ok, I'm here, what's the matter? You look like you've

seen a ghost."

"You're not far off with that Charlie." Zee said frantically. "Here, take this and keep it safe ok." He stuffed the gem into my pocket and turned back around to see out of the alleyway and into the streets. "Charlie, this *is* the real gem ok. Whatever happens, I need you to just play along with me ok, don't question anything, do as I say and most importantly, I need you to trust me. Promise me Charlie."

"Uh, Of course, I promise. Wha—"

Then I saw them. LINGER agents, the only people here in black and red outfits, a giant L imprinted on their right arms. They stuck out like a porcupine in a nudist colony. If these guys made any effort to just blend in, they might actually be hard to avoid.

"Don't move a single muscle." The deep raspy voice came from behind us in the alley.

"Shit!" Zee whispered. "Play along, remember." We both slowly turned around to face three men, all dressed in the customary LINGER onesies and holding automatic rifles which were pointed right at our heads.

"What a pleasant surprise," Zee clapped his hands together and smiled at the nervous agents who looked as though they were ready to fire at any time.

"We aren't here for your games Zee. Time is up and the Director has demanded both of you to be apprehended, dead or alive I should point out too." One of them spoke, raising his firearm up to aim at Zee.

"Okay, okay, I'm not here to argue with you fine people." Zee raised his hands in surrender, "But you should know that, whatever you think we've done, it is all my doing. It was me who dragged Charlie into all of this nonsense." He lowered one of his arms down onto my shoulder. "So, if anyone is to be arrested, it should just be me." Zee was definitely good at talking. But something told me this had absolutely zero chance of working.

"That is not happening you petulant little scumbag. You both are coming along with us back to the moon-base where you will most likely spend the rest of your days behind radiation bars." The leader said, signalling his men move forward and cuff us.

"I'm sorry." Zee mouthed to me as the cold steel clamp was tightened around my wrists.

"I'm going to the moon?" I mouthed back to him. Zee gave me a smile and a raised eyebrow as if to tell me there is nothing for me to be scared of.

The two agents that cuffed us and stood right behind us, making sure we didn't make a run for it, which we actually had no intention of doing at all, while the leader of the outfit placed a small round object on the floor between us and took a few steps back.

"New toy?" Zee asked.

"It's a prototype actually. It's pretty much the same as a kronometer but instead of sending the wearer through the spacetime portals, it opens up a portal right here, so in theory we can simply just step into it." The agent said while pressing various buttons on a little remote he was holding.

"Have you read the instructions?" Zee asked, not sarcastically at all.

The agent raised his head up from this device and looked towards the two agents behind us. "Were there instructions for this thing?"

The two agents looked at each other and just shrugged.

He continued to frantically push buttons. Clearly this was his first time using this device. "Ah! Here we go." The small round device on the floor lit up while making a whizzing noise and I noticed a wind picking up from behind us flowing towards the device. Then there was a loud bang and a flash of light, revealing a swirling round portal sitting in the alleyway in front of us, the wind howled through our hair and flowed directly into the portal as if it was trying to suck everything into it.

"Impressive!" Zee shouted towards the lead agent. "You're sure this thing leads to the moon-base, and not some god forsaken planet in the middle of the Milky Way where we will be permanently slaves of giant turtles and be made to suck on lemons for the rest of our days?"

"Shut up Zee! You're first." The agent gestured towards the two agents behind us to walk us through the portal.

"Wait a sec, I still have a few more questions on my lis—," Zee was cut off as one of the agents shoved him into the swirling circle of doom and immediately jumped in behind him.

"You next," He said, while gesturing a finger at my chaperone, who happily obliged and gave me a violent shove. I shut my eyes and held my breath as if I was jumping into a freezing cold swimming pool for the first time.

FOURTEEN

AD 2775 - August 8 - Zee

I've spent quite a few days in my life in various cells or holding areas within the different locations and bases that LINGER have scattered all over the planet. But this one was different. This one was much more like a prison, this time it felt like they actually meant business. I felt the confidence I had in dealing with this outfit starting to drain out of me. The only thing I knew Charlie and I had on our side was that we had the gem. The problem was, they knew it.

Our cell was small, dark and smelt like old socks. The metal bars usually found on prison cells were replaced with vertical blue lasers. The kind of lasers that looked like they would slice a person into perfectly clean slices at the slightest touch.

"Tell me this is the plan Zee." Charlie said, who was sitting directly next to me on the cell bed, our shoulders touching.

I looked up at the camera on the ceiling which was clearly watching us. "To be honest, at this point I really don't know Charlie." I scratched my head. "They know I have the gem and will be here any second to take it from me."

"Ok, so what are they going to do with it once they take it?" Charlie quietly asked, appearing slightly scared of knowing the answer to his question.

"They will either do nothing with it, you know, maybe admire its shininess and put it on a shelf somewhere so people can check out how pretty it is. Or, they can use it to destroy planets at will. Take a guess as to which one mate." I said to my other self, knowing full well I had to be somewhat clever about the words I was saying.

"My life used to be so peaceful." Charlie said quietly. "I never had to worry about time bending vortexes on the way into the office, or armed agents from the distant future trying to kill me while I went to the loo. Everything about my life was wonderfully boring. How does my hair look today? Did anyone notice me tripping over the pavement? Am I being judged for eating a burrito at lunch for the third day running? Am I going to be reprimanded for being 4 minutes late for work? But now I'm so far away from all of that it's truly mind bending. "Charlie paused.

"But at least if my life is about to come to an end, it wasn't because I refused to mind that gap on the London Underground, or because I fell off my chair and broke my neck. No, it was because I was trying to save the universe. Isn't that something," Charlie said as he turned to me.

"I'm really sorry Charlie. It wasn't my intention to send us into certain death." I would apologise a thousand times if I had the time, because it is my fault we are in this mess.

"But you know what." Charlie said turning to face the laser bars. "I would do this again and again a million times over because I got the chance to meet myself in person. I mean who gets to do that? Who really gets to know themselves truly? You gave me everything Zee, for that I can't ever repay you or thank you enough. You don't ever need to apologise to me."

"Hey Charlie, how about the time I knocked you unconscious? Want me to apologise for that?" I said, smiling.

"Come to think of it. Yes! Say sorry you bastard!" Charlie laughed, suddenly noticing some activity outside the cell.

"The gem Zee, hand it over to me." Colonel Fairservice called, spoiling the moment. He opened up a small hatch beside the laser bars.

"Colonel, what makes you think I have the gem? The agents in Berlin removed it from me." I said, trying and failing to convince Fairservice that his agents were remotely competent.

"I'll ask one more time Zee, the gem, now."

I looked at the Colonel for a moment, realising that I would be wise to comply. I reached into my outside pocket and pulled out the gem. The bright blue laser bars made it glisten brilliantly, slowly, I placed the gem into the open hatch by the bars which shut aggressively once it sensed an object inside it.

"Thank you Zee, that was a rare wise decision you just made." Fairservice said removing the gem from the hatch. He opened his mouth as if to say something else, but shut it back up immediately as he noticed there were some incoming footsteps.

"The gem Colonel, where is the gem?" Director asked impatiently as he approached Fairservice, Kate was following closely behind him.

"Yes, sir, I have it. Here it is." Fairservice swiftly handed it over to him.

The Director held the gem in between his thumb and middle finger, raising it towards the light, seemingly scrutinising every millimetre of it.

"The blue asteroid gem. At last!" He said, giving a satisfied smile. "You can go ahead and prep the weapon Kate." He said, handing the gem over to her. Kate had clearly been trying her hardest to avoid eye contact with me but completely failed miserably.

"Y—, yes sir," Kate replied, and marched off in the opposite direction.

"Uh, Director sir, if I may, did you mention a weapon?" Fairservice asked, taking a small step backwards and looking very confused.

"Colonel, please just ensure the two prisoners are well secured. Let's not have these criminals ruining any more of our plans hey." Director patted on Fairservice on the top of his head while staring directly at me, then walked away in the same direction as Kate.

Colonel Fairservice stood motionless staring into space, still trying to process what he had just heard.

"Colonel—" I started, but was stopped by a furious wave of his hand.

"Don't Zee. Just don't." He looked at me for a millisecond, as if pondering on what next to say, then continued with gritted teeth.

"I gave you the benefit of the doubt Zee, I was the only one trying everything in my power to believe that you were just being a nuisance. Which I get, it's understandable considering the death of Winston." He gave a bitter laugh. "But Jesus, all this time you were back stabbing us from every direction, not only this, you also dragged your old self along for the ride. Well, I hope it was fun while it lasted as I'm sure they have something you fully deserve in store for you." He gave Charlie a pitiful stare, who just looked at the floor. "Good day to you both." The Colonel turned around to leave.

"Colonel please," I was begging now. "You know me. You know I wouldn't do all this for no other reason than just pure bitterness, you know this. The director is planning on vaporising the neighbouring colonised planets with the FTL materials. It's not being used for any sort of intergalactic travel at all. Whatever the Director is telling you, he's lying. He's lying John. You heard it for yourself, *prep the weapon*" I said, pleading for his attention.

Fairservice stopped in his tracks. "Why should I believe

you, when all you've done so far is deceive me," Fairservice turned back to face me, waiting for my next answer.

"If blue asteroid gem is used by the Director and Kate to complete the FTL weapon, then billions of lives will be lost. Colonel you have the opportunity right now to stop this. Simply doing nothing and leaving us here achieves nothing except mass murder perpetuated by that mad man. You can't have this on your immortal conscience John, forever is a very very long time." I felt I was getting through to him." You know deep down that this man is a twisted murderer. If you let this happen you will be complicit in murderous plans. Could you deal with the anguish of watching innocent souls be slaughtered in cold blood for nothing more than bitter vengeance and power?"

I've always known Colonel Fairservice had a good heart, that's precisely why he always saw the good in me, even when no one else did.

"Say what you're saying is true Zee. There is nothing I can do by myself to prevent any of this." He said, with defeat laced within his voice.

"That's right Colonel, there is nothing *you* can do to prevent any of this. But there is something *we* can do to stop it." I stroked my chin, mimicking his serious demeanour. "So, you can start out by deactivating these ridiculous James Bond lasers and we can stop this madness together John." I pulled Charlie closer to me. "Lead us to wherever we need to be to get our hands back on that gem and I will take over from there."

Colonel Fairservice stood there, staring at the both of us like we were completely mad. "Ok Ok, I'll do it, but I can't come with you. You'll have to take your chances with this on your own. The best I can do is at least give you boys a chance." He began to tap his finger in the side of the cell, presumably keying some kind of code to shut down those lasers.

"Colonel John Fairservice, you are my hero on the other side." I said, elated that he had turned his thinking around and now it seemed, he was firmly on our side.

The blue lasers crackled and fizzled out of existence. John stepped aside looking at me intensely. "Don't make me regret this Zee!"

"Quite the opposite John, quite the opposite," I said turning to Charlie, who stood up and ready to move. "Remember what I said." I whispered to Charlie .

"I remember." He said calmly.

"All right then" John started, "go down this corridor until you reach a large red door on your left, there will be a keypad on the right hand side of it. 750718X is the code you need to input. Once inside you will actually be in an elevator. It will take you up to the FTL control room automatically."

"Got it. Let's go Charlie." I said as we sprinted down the corridor.

FIFTEEN

AD 2775 - August 8 - Charlie

"You got that code right Zee?" I said frantically as we came to the large red door.

"Yeah course I do! It's 17087—" Zee stopped and looked up as the door code was written on the ceiling, though knowing LINGER. I honestly wouldn't be at all surprised.

"7-5-0-7-1-8-X, that immortality serum starting to get to your memory hey Zee? He only told us the code about eight seconds ago." I said while keying in the code myself.

Nothing happened.

"Nothings happening!" Shouted Zee in a panic. "Shit, he's double crossed us! Bloody LINGER agents, they are all the same. I can't believe I trusted him to let us go and do this ourselves. I'm such a goddam id—"

The door opened.

"Yes! What did you do Charlie you genius?" Zee said

giving me a huge hug.

"I pressed ENTER." I said calmly.

Zee let go and gave a hysterical laugh. "Like I said. Genius!" He said, flicking my forehead.

One of Mozart's classics sounded out from inside the elevator. I couldn't help but imagine the Director swaying around the control room to it, while putting his evil strategy into play. I've obviously been watching too much television.

The Elevator stopped with a jolt, sending the both of us into a brief panic.

"I think we are here." I said nervously. "Shouldn't the door open though?"

Zee backed up to the other side of the elevator and took a small run up towards the door crashing into it so hard it came clean off its hinges, sending him flying into the room on the other side. We were obviously in the right place as we could see the Director standing over a console to the side of a small glowing stand in the centre of the room. Kate was at the centre stand placing the gem into some sort of clasping device.

The Director turned nonchalantly towards us. "Nice of you

to join the party, boys." He paused to gather his thoughts. "In all my years of dealing with you and that traitor Fairservice, I have to say I was fully expecting this little visit. I'd say come in, but you seemed to have already figured that part out." The director said with complete calmness in his voice. "There is room for all of us in here to enjoy this little party. Welcome." He began to hum to the still playing Mozart tune, raising both his arms, and swirling them in circular motions as if conducting an orchestra.

I took a moment to glance around the room, the first thing that stuck me was the view out of the window which encircled the entire room. We must have been well over a kilometre above the moon, that elevator must have had some serious speed on it, as we can't have been inside it for more than twenty-seconds or so. There were two guards standing at either side of the room, both of whom seemed to be completely unarmed apart from a small metal stick strapped to their sides. Underneath the windows were holographic consoles which followed the room all around, except for the right hand side, which appeared to be some sort of air lock. The blue asteroid gem was sitting in the centre stand and strangely it appeared to be in two different positions at once. The light coming into the gem from underneath it changed its colour and direction. The light was bending and moving, making the ceiling of the room resemble a fantastical three dimensional light show from a Muse gig. It was truly a beautiful sight to behold.

"The refractive index is about 5.990-6.110" Kate began, "the double retractive index is 3.287 and falling, so I've had to do a triple index re-ordering in order to get its true light refraction which is now 0.351. Stable enough to be absorbed by the asteroid." Kate read from the pad she held on her arm to the Director.

"Meaning you can send the beams towards the asteroid and pull it in the direction of our target, correct Commander?" The Director sounded ecstatic, yet still extremely calm.

"This is correct sir." Kate said, much less ecstatic.

"Then get it done already!" The director shouted. In an instant he was like a crazed madman.

"Wait!" Fairservice shouted, bursting into the control room, causing everyone to stop in their tracks. "What are you doing?! I mean, what exactly have you planned for the FTL materials Director?" Using the correct abbreviation for the first time.

"Well well, Colonel Fairservice." The director said dramatically. "Firstly, seize him!" He shouted towards the guards while pointing directly at Colonel Fairservice. The guards leapt into action and were on him in seconds, restraining him against the wall beside the Director, who was now pacing around the room. "I intend to send off this stone," he brought up a hologram of an asteroid, presumably one relatively nearby us, "to Mars and Venus, at a such speed that it would likely vaporise most of the planets in a twinkle of an eye, sending the government and the world orders to unrecoverable chaos. And this is the juicy part, Fairservice." He rubbed his palms together in delight, like a man who just hit jackpot. "They will have no choice but to ask us for help. They will beg us for it. Of course, being the kind and compassionate man that I am, help would be sent at the first opportunity. In return, all control of the solar system is handed over to me. Who can say any fairer than that? Today really is about to be the greatest day in the long history of LINGER" The director gushed.

"The greatest day in the future of the universe!" Zee yelled as he sprinted towards the centre stand that was holding the gem and took a flying leap forwards, grabbed the gem in mid air, landing in a heap right in front of the air lock.

With the guards still occupied with Colonel Fairservice, he had time to pick himself up and move slowly backwards until he could go no further, as he had backed into the door with the words AIR LOCK above it. Zee glanced at me and back at the Director, raising the gem slowly above his head with one hand, and hovering over the PUSH TO OPEN AIRLOCK IN AN EMERGENCY button with the other. Kate seemed to freeze on the spot, as did I. The Events unfolding in the control room seemed to be happening so fast, I felt unable to react and be sure I was making the right decision. Zee said I would know what to do when the time was right. Since I didn't know what to do, I decided that the time probably wasn't right to do anything at all.

"Zee!" The Director called, "You know you don't want this. Put the gem down and give this nonsense up. Opening that door could easily kill your precious friends, I know you wouldn't want that now, would you?" He moved cautiously towards Zee.

Zees' eyes darted to and fro, quickly glancing at everyone in the room, still trying to back up further away from everyone in the room, only ever succeeding in backing into the air lock door.

Like a gunslinger in the wild west, the Director whipped

out his pistol and pointed it straight at Zee. "Now, think about what you are about doing Zee. Think about how wonderful the universe would be if we succeed with this project. We can do this together Zee, you'll see, it will be a beautiful utopia." The Director began to slowly walk towards Zee, still keeping his weapon firmly pointed at his head.

"Have you considered the billions of innocent people that you are going to kill with this act of universal terrorism? You'll only be remembered as the man who murdered half the human race." Zee said, standing firm.

"Murder? Zee you do not know the meaning of the word. Do you think they considered my Raquel when they killed her on Venus? Their pure selfishness and greed to build a reactor, with no safety checks, no testing, built by the lowest bidder, in a fraction of the time it should have taken to build to genesis reactor. Is this not murder to you? Is this not murder Zee?!" The Director voice began to shake. I feared he was about to lose control.

He pointed his gun repeatedly at Zee, shaking it vigorously. "Murder is something that is easily avenged though isn't it Zee. Stealing my fathers work, his ideas, his mind and using it for their selfish purposes and giving him nothing." He paused a moment. "That, is not so easy to avenge." The Director then turned towards me. "I know who you are Charlie, You are our Oracle, you are a deity to LINGER. You are the grandfather of all of this." He turned his attention back towards Zee. "This is our chance Zee! To take back control! Why did you think I let Winston bring you back from your timeline Zee? Winston told me someone from my lineage would better understand the importance of this project. Don't let years of all we worked for go to waste."

Zee stared at the Director for a brief moment. "I'm sorry." He said, raising his hand directly over the airlock button.

A loud bang and a bright white flash echoed through the control room, as Zee fell to the floor with the gem still firmly in his hand, blood seeping out from his chest.

"Zee! No!!" I shouted as loud as I could, feeling the rage rush up from my feet to the top of my head. His eyes were still open and looking directly at me as he gave me a small wink and muttered the words. "You know what to do," before his eyes fell closed and his head slumped forwards.

The Director saw his moment and ran over to where Zee was lying to retrieve his beloved gem. I knew now what Zee had meant by his last words. I rushed over towards

Kate at the exact moment the Director had rushed over to Zee and held my hand over another small red button while turning to face the Director, who was still busy prizing the gem from Zees dead fingers when he realised what was about to happen. His face went from pure joy to one of absolute terror.

I slammed my hand on the button. The airlock door flew open and disappeared into the void of space at breakneck speed, taking the Director who was still holding the gem and Zee with it. The force of the suction lifted me off my feet and propelled me towards the open door.

"Grab onto something Charlie! "Kate yelled in the chaos as she clung to a small pillar in the middle of the room.

At the last moment, I felt my hands grip onto something, it was Colonel Fairservice's hand. He had broken free from the guards who had completely lost any kind of enthusiasm for keeping him restrained.

"Hang on tight Charlie! I've got this." Fairservice yelled, who was holding onto a small broken pipe which was sticking out of the one of the consoles. He stretched his leg out towards the air lock button and smashed it with the top of his foot. The emergency door hatch shut with a deafening thud, the wind subsided and we all dropped to the floor.

I picked myself up and stood by the window to see if I could see anything. Sure enough I could see two figures floating away from us. One of whom was the best friend I ever had. The wave of sadness came over so fast that I had to sit back down on the floor, head in my hands.

SIXTEEN

AD 2775 - August 8 - Charlie

My legs had given in as I sat motionless on the floor, watching the medics who had been called in by Kate who were tending to Colonel Fairservice and the two guards who had taken on a few bruises while the air lock door was open. I was lost in my own world, where do I go from here? How can I carry on without Zee?

Memories came flooding into my mind, The note in the cafe, our first jump together, or rather my first jump with a little shove from him. Meeting Socrates, Plato, Hekate and the Spartan adventures, We sailed the Titanic together and had a drink with one of the greatest men ever to live on planet earth.

I felt a soft pat on my shoulder, "hey," it was Kate. "Can I join you?"

"Uh, Yea, sure." I looked over at the floor area beside me.

"There's plenty of room for two, make yourself at home."

"Listen Charlie, I know you must think I was always in on the Directors plan to cause so much devastation. To some extent you would be correct, but there wasn't anything I could have done to stop him. I mean, I guess what I'm trying to say is that I just didn't have the courage to even try. Zee did have that courage. He was the only one who saw the clear picture of what was actually going on here and the only one with the determination to go out and dedicate his life to stop it." Kate said, as she put her arm fully around my shoulder. "Charlie, you are that person. You did this, you have set our path on a new direction, a direction that will benefit all of human kind. You should be proud of yourself Charlie. I am."

We sat there in silence for a short while until Colonel Fairservice walked back into the control room. I hadn't even noticed he had left in the first place, I assume he had left with the medics when they deemed everyone was ok. It was always obvious that he had a huge soft spot for Zee, despite Zee's general obnoxious behaviour towards him, he was always calm, and never let Zee really ever get the better of him. In some way Colonel Fairservice looked up to Zee, for his personality, his bravery and most of all, his sheer determination to do what is right.

The Colonel rested his hands on the centre console and let out a big puff of breath. "What, has just happened? Charlie, I am so sorry. I was blinded by everything I thought this organisation stood for. I was utterly deceived by the Director all these years." Fairservice began to pace around the room soliloquising. "Zee is a hero, in every sense of the word. A true hero, the guy gave his life to save us all." He turned his attention to the window. "The gem is out there somewhere, I'm not sure whether it's molecular integrity will survive too long being in the harshness of outer space. Which means, while there is now zero danger of the colonies on Mars and Venus being wiped out, we don't have the capability to continue on with the drives that will ensure human kinds survival indefinitely. They say good news comes with bad news and vice versa, but this is most surely a big setback for us."

You'll know what to do. Zee's words began to loop inside my mind again, when it struck me. It hit me like a bolt of lightning shooting through my body. I jumped up from the floor and hurried over to the Colonel.

"Sir."

The Colonel turned to face me. "You don't ever need to call

me sir, Charlie. My name is John, call me John, please."

"Of course, John, sir." I cleared my throat, as I moved closer towards him my hand deep inside my left outside pocket. "John, the molecular integrity of the blue asteroid gem is absolutely fine."

The Colonel raised an eyebrow. "Oh? How could you possibly know this?"

I slowly opened my hand in front of him to reveal a blue shimmering piece of space rock. "Because it's in my hand."

John stared down at the gem, his eyebrows furrowed, then turned back towards the window and immediately back to the gem. "How the— There's two?!"

"Not two John, just one, this one, the gem that left the premises with the Director was a very clever replica that Zee had created some time ago in Sri Lanka. He had already hidden the real gem in Eastern Europe in the eighties." I pointed out the window in the direction of the now vanished fake gem. "That thing was never going to destroy anything except itself. This gem is *the* blue asteroid gem. Please, take it, use it for the right reasons." I opened my palm as far as it would go.

John took the gem from my hand and immediately threw

himself onto me giving me the biggest bear hug I'd had since well, ever. "You boys are unbelievable! I don't know how to thank you."

"It's okay—." I discreetly managed to pry his arms off of me to avoid further strangulation damage.

"I promise you, Ze—, uh sorry Charlie, this gem." He raised it up above his head. "And the technology that it allows, will be handed to the right authorities, to ensure humanity's greatest chance at achieving success with it, with the safety of humans is our absolute top priority."

"That's exactly what Zee would have wanted. That's what he fought and died for. But what will LINGER do now they don't have the Director?" I asked, genuinely interested in how it will continue without someone running the place. I moved over towards one of the windows to get a good view the moon and of the magnificence of outer space.

"Trust me, LINGER will not be the same place again without Zee pushing all our buttons and having us chase him around the cosmos." He gave a short laugh. "He died for a cause and will be remembered, no he will be honoured here at LINGER and will always be in our hearts." He said, resting a hand on my shoulder. "As for this organisation moving on without the Director, well this is something for the board of governors to decide. I'm sure there will be inquiries and court cases which will go on for months or even years over all of this. But in the end, I'm confident that we will have someone at the helm who is slightly more sane than the last guy."

I smiled at John, and decided that now would be a good time to return his hug, which he eagerly accepted. "Can I go home now sir?" I whispered in his ear.

Releasing me from his grip, the Colonel gestured to Kate. "Commander, can you see to it that Charlie here is issued with a one-way kronometer please. Oh, and make sure it's completely untraceable too, just in case hey."

Kate walked over towards me and pulled my wrist up towards her. "We will miss you Charlie." She said, placing a kronometer around my wrist. "It's a one way kronometer and will return you back to your timeline. The date and location has already been input."

"Thank you Kate." I said looking down at the device. "So I just press th—."

"You just press the button." She said with a smile. "Just like before."

"Oh, Charlie, before you go and leave us forever." John said walking over to me, "I want you to have this. Think of is as a souvenir." He handed me a small golden lapel pin badge in the shape of a shield which has the letters LINGER embossed on the front of it. "To remind you of your deeds and of the great Zee." He smiled and turn away.

"Good bye" I said quietly before taking a long deep breath, closing my eyes, I pressed the kronometer button.

SEVENTEEN

AD 2019 - May 30 - Charlie

Everything was the same as it was before, the door was hanging off its hinges from the moment the LINGER agents burst through. My shattered back door was half open and creaking in the gentle breeze. For the moment though, I had absolutely no intention of fixing either of them. I felt strongest urge to leave the flat, I needed to go and see the outside for myself, just to prove that I was really home. I opted of course, for the pub just down the street, 'The Albert Arms'. That place was perfect for a one man celebration. I raised my wrist to check the time, the sight of a kronometer gave me a tiny fright. Thankfully it was dead, so I took it off and threw it onto my loveseat. I took another quick look around my flat to see if it really was just how I left it, when I noticed my wallet and phone sitting on the small coffee table. I've just spent three thousand years without a wallet or my phone, I thought to myself. That *has* to be a record. I picked up my phone and shoved it into my inside pocket and opened up my wallet just to check the contents and sure enough, nothing but receipts, just as I left it. I tucked it into my back pocket and made my way through the shattered back door.

I found myself walking down the street, taking in all the wonders that London in 2019 had to offer. Arguments in the streets, traffic jams, big red double decker buses and of course, drizzle. This moment was truly one of the happiest moments in my life. I was unbelievably grateful just to be alive.

"Hello." A random stranger said as I they passed me in the street.

"Hi there," I replied, thinking he was obviously a weirdo and continued on my way to the pub.

"Excuse me sir." A man, probably in his mid thirties was leaning against a shop window, wearing a dark brown coat, a black fedora hat which seemed to cover most of his face and wintery white hair flowing out the back of it. I have to say he looked extremely familiar.

I stopped to face him. "Hi—hey, have we met before?" I asked, lowering my head and squinting to see if I could decipher where and how I've seen this face before.

The man lift his head. "It's possible I suppose, but I don't think we have. I have a something for you, a proposition in fact. Will you allow me to explain?"

The light bulb in my head clicked into brilliant brightness. "Winston!" I approached him and lifted his hat a little further to reveal those bright blue eyes and that tired weathered look from the Three Greyhounds pub in 1969. "It is you! What are you doing here?"

"Charlie, you are in da—."

"Wait wait, don't tell me." I raised my hand and put my thinking finger against my chin. "Yup, I think I know this one. We have made ourselves a very powerful enemy far far into the future. You need me, being the bloodline of the Director of said enemy to join you on time travelling, mind splitting adventure through intergalactic dimensions to save the universe?"

He looked at me in complete disbelief for a split second, then took a step forwards onto the pavement in front of me, still looking at me in some kind of shock.

"We did it." I whispered. "We did it Winston!" I repeated louder, almost laughing as I shook him by his shoulders.

"We did it?" He was still trying to take this in. "We did

it!?" Almost there. "WE DID IT!" There we go.

Winston slumped down onto the pavement breathing a huge sigh of relief, a tear appeared in the well of his eye, and ran down his cheek.

I sat down and pulled myself up close to him. "There is just one thing that I'm struggling to understand in all of this." I said.

"What's that Charlie?" Winston said, wiping his eyes and sniffing.

"Since I have been told on numerous occasions that you cant change the past, no matter how hard you might try, right?" I began.

"Correct."

"So, how on earth could I be the beginning of the bloodline leading all the way up to the Director of LINGER if the immortality serum you injected me with when we first me has made me infertile?" This was the question that I need an answer for desperately. "Surely, the mere act of me taking the serum means that LINGER will never even exist."

"Oh, that," Winston laughed. "Charlie my boy," he patted me on my shoulder. "The only answer I can give you to that is. You can't change the past. No matter how hard you try." He said, looking at me reassuringly.

"How helpful, thanks Winston," I turned to face the street, tossing an imaginary pebble towards the road.

"So Winston, I was headed to the pub over there across the street. You could join me for a pint if you like. You know, to celebrate the world not ending and all that." I asked.

Winston shook his head. "I would Charlie, but there is something I have to attend to." Just like a hologram being switched off at the mains, he vanished.

"Woah! Well, that was a new one." I said to myself cheerily.

As I sat there on the pavement on that cool, drizzly London afternoon, I remember that I had also picked up my phone from the table at home. I pulled it out of my inside pocket and unlocked the screen. 8% charge still, result!

I tapped on the power button and there was a notification from Noelle. Wow, I thought to myself, that only took three millennia.

I could feel my heart begin to race as I looked at the notification message displaying her name. As much as I didn't want to admit it to myself, I really did miss her.

Sweet memories of her lingered everywhere in my small flat. Maybe, just maybe, I could try explaining to her everything that's happened, even if she'll thinks I've gone bonkers, it would be worth it just to try.

With a little spark of hope in my mind, I tapped open the notification message to read it.

Charlie, we need to talk. Perhaps we could meet in the lovely coffee shop you took me to on our first date?

My jaw fell open and my phone slipped out of my hand and fell to the floor. I was dizzy, nauseous, my stomach was churning around like an over loaded tumble dryer when I read the next line…

…I'm pregnant.

Printed in Great Britain
by Amazon